Edward Marston

On a Sunshine Holyday

Edward Marston

On a Sunshine Holyday

ISBN/EAN: 9783744746335

Printed in Europe, USA, Canada, Australia, Japan

Cover: Foto ©Andreas Hilbeck / pixelio.de

More available books at **www.hansebooks.com**

ON A SUNSHINE HOLYDAY "

PLOVER'S BARROWS.

"On a Sunshine Holyday"

BY

THE AMATEUR ANGLER

" Meadows trim with daisies pied,
Shallow brooks, and rivers wide."
L'Allegro.

LONDON
SAMPSON LOW, MARSTON AND COMPANY
Limited
St. Dunstan's House
FETTER LANE, FLEET STREET, E.C.
1897

CHISWICK PRESS:—CHARLES WHITTINGHAM AND CO.
TOOKS COURT, CHANCERY LANE, LONDON.

My dear Dorothy,

T is thirteen years since I dedicated my first volume to your cousin Lorna, who was then an enthusiastic angler, nearly three years old, and who fished in Dovedale with my walking stick for her rod, two yards of twine for her line, a bent pin for her hook, and a battered tin minnow for her fish. You and she, and Kathleen, and many other of your brothers and cousins, my grandchildren, boys and girls, are now old enough to criticise my style both of fishing and writing from the superior standpoint of youth. I admit at once that you can all do much better than I can, so I beg you not to be very severe in your criticism. Complying with your special request, I am pleased to dedicate this my last book to you, and to express the hope that you and your cousins—a round score—now in the heyday of girlhood and boyhood, may grow up to be good men and women.

E. M.

London,
November, 1897.

by many friends, and by the public, and my gratitude is due to them. This kindness and generosity has led me once again to put together my occasional contributions to "The Fishing Gazette"; and so, with some alterations and additions, to form a volume of similar dimensions, I fear not better, I hope not worse, than its predecessors. I am well aware that from the standpoint of "literature" these papers possess no claim for a separate existence. What I have written has been for me a pleasant occupation of leisure moments, and if to read this volume affords as much pleasure to my friends and my friendly critics as its predecessors seem to have done, I shall be fully rewarded.

The chapters are not all about fishing, for I had but few fishing excursions to record; the chief connection between them is that all have reference, more or less, to "sunshine holydays."

E. M.

CONTENTS.

CHAP.		PAGE
I.	WOODPECKERS AND VIPERS	2
II.	HAMPSTEAD HEATH ON A BANK HOLIDAY	11
III.	"TALES FROM THE TELLING HOUSE" .	21
IV.	SALISBURY PLAIN AND THE VALLEY OF THE AVON	30
V.	MAY FLY FISHING ON THE ITCHEN (1896)	38
VI.	"ANIMALS AT WORK AND PLAY" . .	44
VII.	ROUND AND ABOUT LOWESTOFT . . .	55
VIII.	THE PROSE OF FLY FISHING	65
IX.	A BIBLIOGRAPHY OF GILBERT WHITE .	74
X.	"THE COMPLEAT ANGLER"	80
XI.	OUR MAY FLY OUTING ON THE TEST (1897)	88
XII.	OUR MAY FLY OUTING ON THE ITCHEN (1897)	97
XIII.	AUGUST BANK HOLIDAY FISHING (A SINGULAR AND CURIOUS INCIDENT)	103
XIV.	ON THE EDGE OF EXMOOR	110
XV.	THE DOONE VALLEY	125
XVI.	"FAMILIAR WILD BIRDS"	137

LIST OF ILLUSTRATIONS.

		PAGE
PLOVER'S BARROWS . . . . . . *frontispiece*		
LESSER SPOTTED WOODPECKER . . . *to face*		4
VIPERS (*Vipera Aspis L.*) . . . . . . ,,		10
VALE OF HEALTH, HAMPSTEAD HEATH . ,,		12
THE WATER SLIDE, BADGERY WATER . ,,		24
BUTCHER BIRDS. . . . . ,,		32
STONEHENGE (THE TRILITHON) . . . . ,,		34
THE EUROPEAN BADGER (*Meles taxus*) . ,,		48
THE BEACH, LOWESTOFT . . . . . . ,,		56
IZAAK WALTON'S MARRIAGE CHEST . . ,,		86
DULVERTON . . . . ,,		110
OUR DIGGINGS . . . . ,,		112
THE BUZZARD . . . . ,,		114
LANDACRE BRIDGE . . . . ,,		118
KESTREL . . . . ,,		136
CREEPER . . . . ,,		138

"ON A SUNSHINE HOLYDAY."

CHAPTER I.

WOODPECKERS AND VIPERS.

NE of the consequences of the publication of my little book, "By Meadow and Stream," is that I have been dubbed a *naturalist*—a title to which I beg to be permitted to say I have no claim whatever.

Some of my friends have got the impression that I know all about every bird, insect, or reptile to be found on this island. I thought I had sufficiently guarded myself against this too flattering assumption by stating that my experience and my life amongst birds and beasts began and ended nearly sixty years ago. Since then my lot has been cast rather among unfeathered bipeds and four-footed creatures of the canine and feline species. I have found neither time nor opportunity for studying nature beyond what is left of it in a pretty but city-haunted suburban garden.

The late Sir Richard Owen was able, owing to his great genius and life-long experience, to construct a whole antediluvian animal of megatherium dimensions from a single bone or tooth. In like manner have I been called upon to construct a bird from a few feathers.

A good lady, who had done me the honour of reading my book, sent me not long ago, from the neighbourhood of Abergavenny, a small shattered wing of a bird, which her cat had killed and mangled in her garden. She had never seen a bird like it, and she particularly wished me to tell her what it was. Luckily—by a mere fluke, as it were—I have been able to reconstruct this bird from its few feathers, and to furnish the lady with a perfect description of it. A friend staying with me, of a very observant nature, inquiring mind, and retentive memory, told me that she had seen, only a few days ago, a bird of exactly similar plumage hung up by its beak in a poulterer's shop. She inquired what the bird was; it was there clearly for show rather than for gastronomic purposes; she was told that it was a *woodpecker*.

Now, if there is one bird of the rarer kind that I thought I remembered better than any other, it is a woodpecker. I have seen lots of them in

the woods and orchards on the old farm in the
days of old, and I am quite sure that I have
never seen one since ; but surely, unless my
memory has sadly played me false, all my woodpeckers were *green*, with a bit of red on their
heads, and three times the size of the bird which
this wing represents, and which is not much
larger than a sparrow's wing, and it is striped
black and white. This, of course, will sufficiently
show the extent of my ornithological knowledge.
I had only seen one species, and supposed there
was one only. I turned to Gilbert White, but,
to my surprise, the woodpecker is not indexed
in my edition, and the only reference I could
find is that he appears about Michaelmas, and
disappears about April.

Bewick, however, is more informing. He not
only tells me that there are three kinds, the
" green," the " greater," and the " lesser spotted "
—the latter he calls the *barred woodpecker*—he
says the smallest of the three is only five inches
and a half in length ; weight nearly one ounce,
and that the crown of the head is *crimson*. He
furnishes a lovely little woodcut of this bird, and,
on comparing it with my wing, I am astonished
at its absolute fidelity—bar for bar, spot for spot.
Every feather is there as distinct as if he had
had this particular wing to copy.

Robert Mudie, author of " Feathered Tribes
of the British Islands," says : " The several

woodpeckers vary in tint with the general
colours of the trees which they select."

Dr. Hamilton, in his delightful book, " The
Riverside Naturalist," describes all three in a
very interesting way. " The green woodpecker,"
he says, "when not too much disturbed, will
take the same round day after day, visiting the
same trees, beginning at the base, and working round and round all up the trunk, searching
for food.   It is especially fond of ants, and hops
in a curious upright position from one ant hill to
another. . . . Its laughing cry has given it the
provincial name of Yaffel.

" The *lesser spotted* woodpecker is more
common than its larger cousin, the *greater
spotted*, and if looked for carefully enough in
the elms and poplars may often be noticed. . . .
It is more barred in the wing, with its back
more white than the greater.   The crown of the
head is red.

" The *greater spotted* is not so common."

Dr. Bull says : " The *great spotted woodpecker*,
though nowhere numerous, is yet not rare in the
oak woods and orchards of Herefordshire.

" The lesser spotted, though not abundant in
Herefordshire, is yet not a rare bird."

R. Bowdler Sharpe says : " The lesser spotted
woodpecker is easily recognized by its lesser
size, being no bigger than a nuthatch.   Both
sexes have the head scarlet."

LESSER SPOTTED WOODPECKER.

Mudie says its prevailing colour on the upper part is black, with dull red on the hind head and partially on the crown.

Thus have these learned authorities taught me to build up my black and white barred and battered wing into a beautiful *lesser spotted woodpecker.* The only difference, if it can be called a difference, between them is that Bewick says the head is crimson, Dr. Hamilton says it is red, R. Bowdler Sharpe says it is scarlet, and Mudie says it is dull red.

In my vagabond school days it was my delight, when not fishing, to stroll off on a spring holiday afternoon into the woods to listen to the birds, for, although I have not a musical ear, and could never whistle or sing a tune properly, yet the songs of many birds have always had a singular charm for me. A number of birds singing their own songs must, I should think, produce on sensitive ears a jarring discord. I suppose I am so far insensible as not to feel the jar, though sensitive enough to find it pleasant harmony.

> " . . . Therefore am I still
> A lover of the meadows, and the woods
> And mountains, and of all that we behold
> From this green earth."

One day I was sitting under a beech in the wood, manufacturing a whistle out of a stem of mountain ash, when I heard a tap, tap, on an oak branch close by.

> " Every leaf was at rest, and I heard not a sound,
> But the woodpecker tapping the hollow oak tree."
>
> MOORE.

There was a beautiful green woodpecker labouring away at the bark with his strong beak, supported by his two front claws, clinging to the tree, and assisted by his strong tail feathers pressed close against the bark. I had never seen one so near before. They are so shy that it is no easy matter to catch them at work. One generally sees them on the wing, flitting from one tree to another, with a peculiar undulating flight : wings spread and flapping for the rise, and closed for the fall. He was chipping off great bits of soft wood—bent on working a hole into the rotten wood to nest in, or else seeking for insects. Mudie informs me that he tries round the tree till he comes to a place which is hollow, and upon that he beats the drum in loud and rolling taps, but yet without in the least perforating the tree ; and the bird contrives to make the sound merry, and in some degree musical, and if his mate catches the sound she answers to it, the bargain is concluded, and the labour of the season begins. This drumming on the tree is, in fact, his love-note— and a summons to his mate that a nest is to be formed and food to be found. When really engaged in boring for nesting purposes the sound is different, and resembles the grinding of a thick piece of steel on a rather smooth stone, and may be heard at a considerable distance.

I asked old Bollington, the parish clerk, who happened to be on his way through the wood, what he called the bird : "Why," says he, "that's a *hickle*, and he's tapping for rain." Old B. was an excellent clerk, and said "Aamen" with sonorous dignity, but he was too fond of wandering down the steep of that wood to the village pub. below. He went, unhappily, once too often, for not long after my interview he was found dead on a Sunday morning in a quarry in the wood near to the path, into which he had fallen on his return from the pub.

VIPERS AND ADDERS.

Are they identical ? Do they bite, and do they sting ? Truly, a little knowledge is a dangerous thing. I am clearly getting beyond my depth in discussing this grave question.[1] I turn to my Gilbert White, and he solemnly tells me : " Providence has been so indulgent to us as to allow of only one venomous reptile of the serpent kind in these kingdoms, and that is the *viper.*'

---

[1] Previously referred to in " By Meadow and Stream."

He does not use the word adder, but, of course, he means it.   That was a source of some comfort to me, but on turning over the leaves of Wm. Howitt's "Year Book of the Country," to see if he has anything to say about woodpeckers, I came across the following remarks, which compel me to offer another apology to Mr. Van Dyke, the author of "Little Rivers," for whose benefit, it will be remembered, that I quoted Scripture to prove that he was wrong about adders stinging.   And "Cotswold Isys" quoted Scripture to prove that I was wrong.[1]

"In the midst of the thickets we had nearly trodden upon a viper two feet three inches long, black as ink, which we killed.   It would appear that we have in this country (these kingdoms, G. White says) two species of venomous snakes : the black kind, and the lesser red-brown kind, or adder, found on the sunny heaths.   The woodman said that this owed its deep jet blackness to its recent change of skin.   Perhaps so ; but this was evidently of a totally different kind to the brown adder of the moors.   Besides its intense inky colour *and its poison fangs in the mouth, it had a sting in its tail!*

"The keeper, to whose house we took it, pronounced it of the most venomous kind."

Dr. Hamilton ("Riverside Naturalist") says

---

[1] See "By Meadow and Stream."

we have only one venomous snake in the country, and that, although the bite of an adder will cause very unpleasant symptoms, he believes there is no record of death being caused by it among the human race. As a boy I have killed dozens of adders when I have found them basking on sunny banks. The proper method I was told was to lash them on the tail first with a pliant ash or hazel switch. My method was to strike on the tail first and then thrash away as fast as I could ply the stick indiscriminately all over the body. The largest I ever killed was about eighteen inches [1]—Dr. Hamilton says that any over twenty-four inches must be considered as great rarities. The best remedy for the bite is ammonia employed both externally and taken internally. They are very easily approached, being as they are said to be deaf, or at least very sound sleepers ; or it may be, as it has been said in

---

[1] I remember about twenty-five years ago, when in Devonshire fishing, I was being driven by a farmer from Exford to Withypool, across a part of Exmoor, when we saw an adder on the road ; the farmer pulled up his horse, jumped off the trap, and went for the reptile, but the latter was too quick for him, and disappeared behind a bush in the bank. The farmer pulled the bush and grass about *with his hands* to try to find the adder, but failed to do so. He told me afterwards that if he had had time to mark a circle round the brute on the road and say a particular verse from the Psalms, the adder could not have moved out of the circle.—R. B. M.

fable, that the adder, to prevent hearing the voice of a charmer, lays one ear on the ground and sticks his tail into the other.[1] [2]

[1] Dr. Brewer's " Dictionary of Phrase and Fable."

[2] One day Bach found the painter Gainsborough fagging at the bassoon. " Nay now," said Gainsborough, " it is the richest bass in the world. Now listen again." " Listen," cried Bach, " I did listen at your door, and by all the powers above, it is just for all the world as the veritable braying of a jackass." " Damn it," retorted Gainsborough, " why, you have no ear, man ; *no more than an adder.*"—MRS. ARTHUR BELL'S *Life of Thomas Gainsborough.*

VIPERS (*Vipera Aspis* L.).

CHAPTER II.

HAMPSTEAD HEATH ON BANK HOLIDAY.

N Hampstead Heath, Easter Bank Holiday begins on Good Friday. As a dweller in Hampstead for some years, I could not help but learn, through the medium of the Press or otherwise, that the Heath on Bank Holidays is largely visited by its owners, its landlords in perpetuity. My impression is that the inhabitants of Hampstead know nothing whatever of these owners or lords of the Heath. Never is rural, quiet Hampstead so absolutely peaceful and quiet, especially that part of it to the west of High Street, as on Bank Holiday. I suppose, as a rule, it moves away to the sea, or is off angling by some pleasant stream, or it goes somewhere far enough off; those who remain shut themselves up in their houses, and keep themselves in intentional ignorance of the crowds of visitors which railways, 'buses, carriages, cabs and carts, horsemen, donkeymen, and footmen pour upon the Heath close by.

I confess that I myself, in all the years of my residence here, have never till now found an opportunity of seeing what this happy hill is like on a Bank Holiday. On such occasions I have generally preferred to hie me away to the water side.

We who reside in Hampstead know well enough what our Heath is like on all other days of the year ; we know that it stands high above, and overlooks the greatest city in the world, and that it is altogether that great city's most charming suburb ; its scenery is exquisite in its wild variety ; its extensive views for many miles on every side are unsurpassed. On all days but Bank Holidays we call it our Heath, and are very proud of it. Yet, why should we be so proud ? It no more belongs to us individually than it does to each individual of the hundred or, may be, two hundred thousands of our brothers and sisters who come from the uttermost parts of London on these rare occasions to pay a visit to their property.

Here are no less than 481 acres of most delightful lands, of hill and dale, copses, ferns, gorse, and ponds, purchased mainly by the people of London at a cost of nearly £360,000. To be precise, I will give exact figures, quoting from that excellent work, " Records of Hamp-

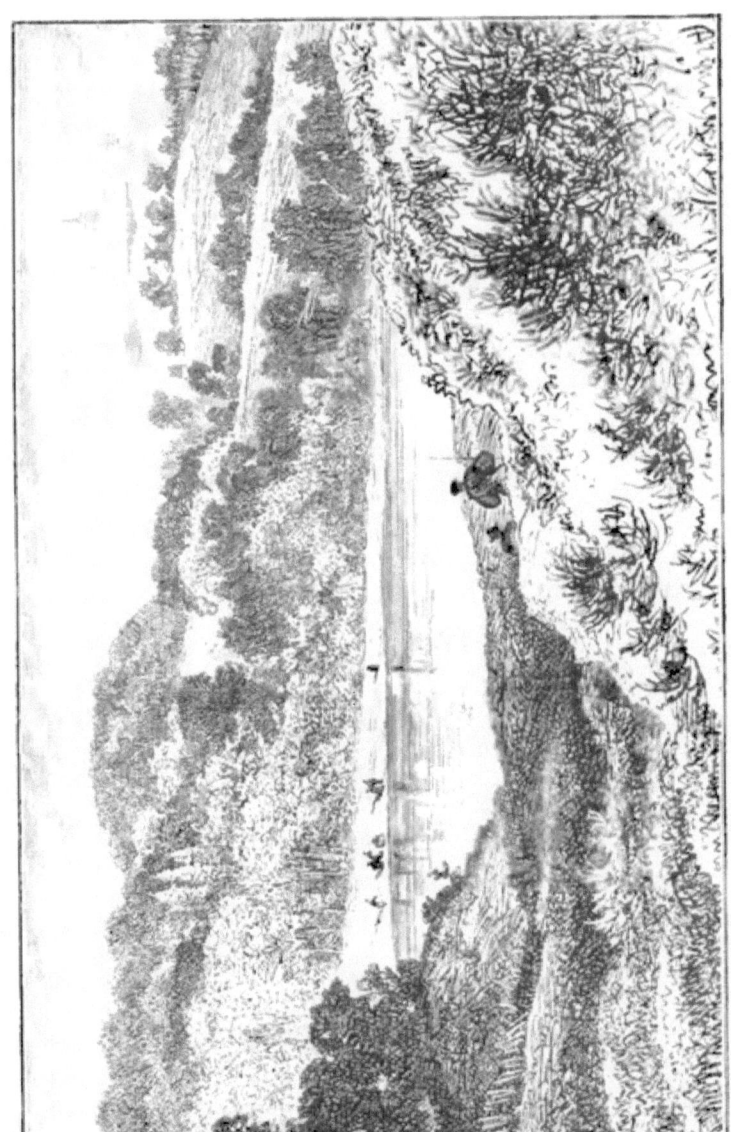

stead," by R. E. Baines, C.B. I learn that the East and West Heaths, comprising 220 acres, were purchased in 1869 from the lord of the manor, Sir John Maryon Wilson, by the Metropolitan Board of Works for the sum of £57,000 ; and in 1889 Parliament Hill Fields and the Brickfields, comprising 261 acres, were acquired and paid for as follows :

London County Council	£151,000
City Parochial Charities	50,000
Vestries : St. Pancras	30,000
Hampstead	20,000
St. Marylebone	5,000
Raised by public subscriptions . .	46,000
	£302,000
Add cost of East and West Heaths .	57,000
	£359,000

These figures may be interesting to some readers.

Parliament Hill was formerly better known as Traitors' Hill, for here it was popularly believed that the Guy Fawkes conspirators had assembled to view the blowing up of the Houses of Parliament, Nov. 5, 1605, probably a popular fiction.

This year (1896) the Heath, owing to the very mild winter and favourable weather since, began early to assume its spring mantle of green. The

grass on the East Heath and on Parliament
Hill Fields is lush and long enough to cover
one's feet. Willows, elms, chestnuts, hawthorns,
and all other trees and shrubs are budding and
bursting into leaf and flower. Gorse on the
West Heath is in full bloom.

" The green buds glisten in the dews of spring,
And all is vernal rapture as of old."

KEPLE.

All nature seems flush and ready for the Easter
merry-making.

On Good Friday I was first reminded that
Easter Monday was at hand. Our city proprietors from down Whitechapel way had
already taken possession of their beautiful fields.
Here were many thousands of them, and they
brought with them loads of cocoa-nuts, swings,
and attractions of all sorts; a roaring trade was
going on. On Saturday morning I strolled over
the same ground, and all had vanished. Only
a few swings remained, and these were carefully
tied up, so as not to be played with in the
absence of the proprietors.

On Monday morning, Bank Holiday, I again
visited the same scene, now, as if by magic, all
and a good deal more had returned. From the
railway station, all the way up the hill, past the
Vale of Health, and up to the Spaniards Road
near the flagstaff, the road was lined with long

sheets fixed on poles, forming a background for numberless cocoa-nut shies, and the play was fast and furious. Besides these cocoa-nut contests, what grand sights we saw as we pressed through the crowd. Here was on view "the largest rat that ever was seen," and "two wonderful four-horned sheep, bred on the rugged mountains, imported by a well-known nobleman; very fierce animals, they have been known to kill human beings." Then comes "the mascu-line-feminine-gender girl, who was born with a most beautiful cranium orifice." I don't quite know what a "cranium orifice" is, but assuming that one may take the whole human head as a *cranium*, then doubtless the "orifice" may be taken as the beautiful maiden's mouth—but this is wild conjecture. After this is to be seen "Madame Leonie, the fattest woman in the world; she travelled in the United States with Barnum's show." Close by is the American game of baseball, which, it seems, means throwing balls at the head of a living nigger. This nigger enjoys the fun. His head is protruded through a small aperture in a wooden frame, and the fun, at three shies a penny, is to hit his thick head with an indiarubber ball. "Play up, gents," he shouts, "twenty can shie at me at once, the more the merrier." There are more misses than hits, and he dodges the hits cleverly, so as to receive them on his crown rather than his nose.

Of course, refreshments abound on all sides, but, above all (and this may be interesting to anglers), the air is scented, if not embalmed, with the fragrant odours of frying fish, cooked in rivers of fat over charcoal fires—truly giving forth " an ancient and a fish-like smell."

Swings by the thousand abound all along the line. In one of them I saw, or thought I saw, an old friend enjoying the fun like a young sky-lark. "Up to the sky go we, go we!" he seemed to be singing, and up to the highest height the swing would reach went he. Down again, and up again, his bald head gleaming in the air, his rosy countenance a picture of happiness, and his velveteen coat flaps enjoying the flight. I thought my old friend had gone a-fishing up the Thames. It is just possible that I may have been mistaken, after all, for my sight is not as good as it was.

The steam "merry go-round" at the Vale of Health was kept merrily going all day, and the owner must have made a mint o' money.

Then there were machines for athletes to test their strength by striking a wedge with a beetle or heavy sledge hammer, which sent an indicator up a slotted pole to a number, which told the relative strength of the competitors.

And so I squeezed through the crowd till I came to the most wonderful sight of all, but it did not seem to obtain the patronage it deserved.

It was a show which contained a monster described as an animal *partly man* and *partly pig*. The showman was savage at the stupidity of the passers by. "If," says he, "it was some machine wrought by the hand of man, you would rush to see it ; but here is *not* the work of man ; it is the work of Nature ; it is far more man than pig. A well educated and most intelligent young man you will find him. Go in for one penny, and you will see one of the most remarkable freaks that Nature ever produced."

I may say that, not caring to be "disillusionised," I preferred taking the pictures and statements made outside as correct, without further investigation.

Much as I rejoice in the wild enjoyment of my fellow owners of this beautiful heath on this lovely April day, I am not sorry when I get through the throng of merry makers and reach the Spaniards Road. The West Heath was not crowded with visitors ; it had no attractions in the way of shows and swings and cocoa-nut shies. Still it was well studded here and there with mooning young couples and groups of youths and maidens playing at "kiss in the ring."

Angling in the Hampstead ponds being forbidden, owing to the close time, from March to June, that favourite resort of young and old cockney anglers, the Leg of Mutton pond, was quite deserted.

C

What a very singular aquatic bird is the moor-hen. Down our rivers one cannot approach him within a hundred yards but he dives and is off like a shot ; now here, on this Leg of Mutton pond, a pair of moorhens reared a brood last year, and here I see them now, as tame as barn-door ducks, and yet this pond is a sort of pandemonium for dogs and boys. The birds, it is true, keep to the knuckle end of the pond, amongst the coverts of sedge weeds, and there they seem to be quite unscared by boys or dogs.

I supposed that I was the only angler in that great throng—for who, if he could help it, would choose charms even such as I have tried to describe, rather than wanderings by pleasant rivers ? and yet to my astonishment, as I sauntered quietly up the hill, my ears were assailed by a shout, " Hollo, 'Amateur Angler'! how are you ?" Surely it was *Vox et præterea nihil!* unless indeed it proceeded from the stentorian lungs of " Red Spinner," for on turning round I caught sight of the back of him spinning down the hill at a speed of twenty miles an hour on a bicycle. The delights of cycling must be near akin to angling when such an expert on such a day prefers the former to the latter.

I did not count the owners who came to visit their Heath to-day ; I am therefore unable to say within a few thousands how many there may have been ; if I may be allowed to guess, I should say the number could not be less than two hundred thousand.

How they came, and how they vanished, is a mystery ; but this may truly be said of them, so far as my observation went, and I spent four hours on the ground, they were, considering their numbers, the most orderly, peaceful, law abiding crowd that ever assembled. Surely they presented a fine example of the benefits conferred on the people by the education derived from Board Schools. In fact, if one wanted to be captious, one might almost complain that they seemed to be too good. There was really nothing for the police to do. Think of the glories of Hampstead Heath and the other heaths around London a hundred years ago, and look at them now.

"Are the days then gone when on Hounslow Heath
   We flashed our nags ?
When the stoutest bosoms quailed beneath
   The voice of Bags ?
Ne'er was my work half undone, lest
   I should be nabbed ;
Slow was old Bags, but he never ceased
   Till the whole was grabbed."

                                 Paul Clifford.

Let it not be supposed for a moment that I think that those blood-stirring old times were better than the mild excitements of to-day. But let us think of the difference to these people

between a fine April day, as this Easter Monday
has been, and how that immense throng would
have fared on a pouring rainy day. I am sure
this has been a happy day both for sightseers
and those who provided the sights ; many bushels
full of coppers must have been exchanged
between them, and all retired to their homes in
the far away east and south full of happy experiences which will last them to rejoice over for
many months to come.

CHAPTER III.

"TALES FROM THE TELLING HOUSE."[1]

T is not necessary to introduce the author of "Lorna Doone" to my readers. His great romance is known wherever the English language is spoken; it has become an English classic, and ranks with the best productions of the best writers of romance of the century. As Sir Walter Scott was called the "Wizard of the North," so has R. D. Blackmore been called the "Wizard of the West," for this applies to all the other writings of the same author. It may be in a less degree, for "Lorna Doone" has taken a hold upon all classes of readers, and in quarters where works of imagination are not usually much esteemed. You hear its merits discussed on the top of four-horse coaches—coachman

---

[1] "Tales from the Telling House." By R. D. Blackmore, author of "Lorna Doone."

and guard know all about it. You will find it in
the cottages of the West, where it is treasured
as a work, constantly read and remembered.
"Lorna Doone" to a Devonshire man is as
good as clotted cream, almost.[1] And yet there
are characters, incidents, thrilling adventures,
lovely descriptions of picturesque scenes—prob-
ing with a magic touch the very heart of nature
—to be found in every one of Mr. Blackmore's
romances. What thrilling—one might almost
say blood-curdling—incidents are to be found in
"Clara Vaughan." What bright humour and
droll pictures in "Cripps the Carrier." What
strange adventures in "Cradock Nowell,"
"Christowell," "Alice Lorraine," and "Mary
Anerley," and the rest of them. And the last,
"Perlycross," equals the best.

Anglers all should feel a special and particular
interest in all Mr. Blackmore's books, for in
nearly all of them will be found, interspersed
with matter of more dramatic character, many
very agreeable bits of angling adventures, described in a way no angling writer has ever yet
surpassed.

Even in the tragic story "Slain by the
Doones," which is the first of four stories under
the general title "Tales from the Telling
House,"[2] Mr. Sylvester Ford, the fine old Eng-

[1] Preface to "Lorna Doone," 6th edit.
[2] "The 'Telling-houses' on the moor are rude cots

lish gentleman, who met with such a tragic fate
at the hands of the ruthless Doones, was an
ardent angler.   His daughter, who tells the sad
story, relates that "with a fishing rod made by
himself, and a basket strapped over his shoulder
. . . he set off in the highest spirits, as anglers
always seem to do, to balance the state in which
they shall return."

His Sylvia waited, alas, in vain for his return.

"But the shadows of the trees grew darker,
and the song of the gray-bird died out among
them, and the silent wings of the owl swept by,
and all the mysterious sounds of night in the
depth of forest loneliness, and the glimmer of a
star through the leaves here and there, to tell us
that there still was light in heaven; but of
an earthly father not a sign; only pain, and
long sighs, and deep sinking of the heart."

The squire and his daughter lived all by
themselves in a wood, and trees were the only
creatures near them—some five or six miles
from the Doones' Valley.   The good squire,
notwithstanding the bad reputation of these
gentlemanly Doones, scorned the idea that men
of birth could ever behave like savages.   No
gentleman would ever dream of attacking an
unarmed man, he thought, and so he resolved to
fish the brook which ran away from their strong-
where the shepherds meet to 'tell' their sheep at the end
of the pasturing season."—*Lorna Doone.*

hold, believing that he may see some of them
and have a peaceful interview. And so he wandered through the woods till he came upon the
Badgery water, taking with him Dick Hutchings.
The boy, who was the only witness of what
happened, related how

"Squire had catched a tidy few, and he
seemed well pleased with himself, and then we
came to a sort of a hollow place where one
brook floweth into the other. Here was a casting of his fly, most careful, for if there was ever
a trout on the feed, it was like to be a big one.
Lucky for me, I was keeping round the corner,
when a kingfisher bird flew along like a string-
bolt, and there were three great men coming
round a fuzz-bush.

"'Ho, fellow!' one of them called out to
squire, 'who give thee leave to fish in our
river?'

"'Open moor,' says squire, 'and belongeth to
the King, if it belongeth to anybody. Any of
you gentlemen hold his Majesty's warrant to
forbid an old officer of his?'"

This put them in a dreadful rage, and they
requested him to give up his spoil. The squire
walked up from the pebbles at that and stood
before the three of them.

"'You be young men, but I am old; nevertheless, I will not be robbed by three or by thirty of
you. If you be cowards enough, come on.'"

Then the cowards attacked him ; one of them he slew with the butt end of his fishing rod, and then one of them ran a long blade into squire, "and there he was a lying as straight as a lath, with the end of his white beard as red as a rose."

Then comes a most vivid account of a concerted attack on the Doones by the Devon and Somerset heroes, led on by Colonel Jeremy Stickles. They had mounted their culverins on opposite heights above the Doone Valley, with the intention of pounding the Doones therefrom, when suddenly "An elderly gentleman of great authority appeared among the Somerset Bombardiers. On his breast he wore a badge of office, and in his hat a noble plume of the sea eagle, and he handed his horse to a man in red clothes.

" ' Just in time,' he shouted, ' and the Lord be thanked for that ! By order of his Majesty I take supreme command. Ha, and high time for it. You idiots ! Where are you pointing your guns ? what allowance have you made for windage ? Why, at that elevation you'll shoot yourselves. Up with your muzzles, you yellow jackanapes ! Down on your bellies ! Hand me the linstock ! By the Lord, you don't even know how to touch them off !' "

This was no other than Councillor Doone himself. He had pointed the gun right into the

Devonshire men on the opposite bank, who
promptly returned the fire, the result being that
young Captain Purvis was hit in the breast by a
flat-bottomed bottle, and was carried wounded
into Miss Sylvia Ford's cottage. She nursed
him so well, and felt such pity for his weakness,
" until when the tray came out of his room soon
after one of those pitiful moments, it was plain
. . . that the young man had left very little upon
a shoulder of Exmoor mutton, and nothing in a
bowl of thick onion sauce ; " after such treatment, what could he do but fall in love with
her ?

Readers of " Lorna Doone " will remember
that tremendously exciting scene where John
Ridd, by the aid of Gwenny Carfax, rescued
Lorna from them. It was a considerable time
after that event that this tragedy happened to
the squire—a story, "every word of which is
true, and the stoutest writer of history cannot
make less of it by denial." Carver Doone had
lost his Lorna through the might of John Ridd.
He had heard of the beauty of Sylvia, and had
determined to carry her off to replace his lost
Lorna, and now that he had brutally murdered
her father, he made a fiendish attack upon the
daughter by breaking into her house at mid-
night. How her house was stormed, and how
heroically defended, I will leave readers to find
out. That, and the subsequent carrying off the

young lady, her release by young Purvis, "as
fine a young trooper as ever drew sword," and
the battle on a saddle-backed bridge in a deep
wooded glen, with roaring water under it—in
which John Ridd, with a staff like the stem of a
young oak tree, fought like a giant, is about as
brilliant a bit of descriptive writing as was ever
penned in history or fiction.

One distinguishing characteristic of all Mr.
Blackmore's writings is that they will bear re-
peated readings.   If read a first time in a
hurried and breathless way for the purpose of
following up and unravelling the plot, you will
be astonished on a second and more deliberate
reading to note how much of real beauty of
style and language has been overlooked. You
will find nothing commonplace or slipshod any-
where.   Every sentence has been carefully
thought out and constructed, and the result is
a charm of rhythm which brightens even the
least interesting theme.

"Frida ; or, the Lover's Leap, a Legend of
the West Country," of the time of Charles I., is
the next story—a story full of pathetic interest
which will repay more than one reading on
account of its tragic termination, the interest of
its story, and the poetry of its prose. The Baron
de Wichehalse, around whom and his daughter
the story centres, was doubtless an ancestor of
the Count de Wichehalse who figures largely

both in " Lorna Doone " and in " Slain by the Doones." A recent writer has called it " One of the saddest tales of woman's love and man's leaving that has ever been written."

The next story, " George Bowring," is one of modern life, and tells how the teller of the story and his friend, George Bowring, took a holiday trip into Wales, the one an angler, the other an artist. They found themselves at length at a village called Aber Aydyr, lying under Cader Idris. Here they halted, the one to sketch, and the other to fish.

" Here George put his rod together, and I heard the click of reel as he drew the loop at the end of the line through the rings, and I heard him cry ' Chut !' as he took his flies from his Scotch cap and found a tangle ; and I saw the glistening of his rod, as the sunshine pierced the valley, and then his tall, straight figure pass the corner of a crag that stood as upright as a tombstone, and after that no more of any live and bright George Bowring."

Then the teller tells how poor G. B. was found dead, and how the murderer was discovered twenty years after.

Lastly we come to a real fishing story, and one whose brightness and sparkle, and true sportsmanlike description could only have been written by an accomplished scholar and a man of infinite wit and humour. Read it quietly and carefully, my friends, and do not hasten on to discover whether that big trout was ever pulled out of "Crocker's Hole." You will pick up many a gem of thought and expression ; many a bit of subtle humour, which in a hasty perusal you would miss. Let me tell you again this little book, "Tales from the Telling House," is one to be taken up when you want to be restful and quiet. Take it to a cosy corner and you will find it soothing and pleasant, always piquant and fresh, and never commonplace. It comes from the pen of a master hand. I will not spoil your pleasure by further quotation or comment. I leave you to wander with young Pike in the Devonshire valleys and along the banks of the Culm, and find out the many schemes of this youngster, and whether he succeeded or not in catching that big trout in "Crocker's Hole."

CHAPTER IV.

SALISBURY PLAIN AND THE VALLEY OF THE AVON.

May, 1896.

"Gives not the hawthorn bush a sweeter shade
To shepherds, looking on their silly sheep,
Than doth a rich embroider'd canopy
To kings that fear their subjects' treachery."

King Henry V.

IF in my childhood I ever read that wonderful story by Hannah More, "The Shepherd of Salisbury Plain," I am ashamed to say that I have forgotten all about it ; but I have lately been across a large part of Salisbury Plain, and have seen many a shepherd and many thousands of sheep ; and a pretty sight it is, to see a thousand sheep just released from their pen on the top of the Downs on a hot afternoon rushing helter-skelter down the steep hillsides to the water ; a scene which occurs daily, but which, seen for the first time, seems quite an exciting and picturesque feature in the landscape. The shepherds are a stalwart race of men, as good, I'll warrant, all of 'em, as the particularly good man immortalized by Hannah More.

To pleasure seekers, and all such as care for nothing but their own special amusement, this present month of May must have been wonderfully attractive; it derived from April a fair amount of moisture, for

" April showers prepare the way for May flowers,"

and up to the middle of the month the meadows have preserved a pleasant degree of lush verdure, and plenty of buttercups and daisies ; but now are the croakers beginning to croak, and predict a droughty summer, and lament over it before it comes.

I must own myself to be among the pleasure seekers. A cordial, genial invitation to run down and fish the Wiltshire Avon fetched me at once right off my office stool, and sent me one day last week away by rail and road to attractive, pretty Amesbury. Thereby flows the pleasant Avon. That pleasant river has a great reputation for the abundance and size of its trout, as all you anglers know ; and my genial host is the happy possessor of three miles of it. Your 1 lb. or ½ lb. trout is there looked upon as nought. Notwithstanding the drought of the last fortnight or three weeks, water was plentiful, and weeds abundant. I cannot boast of the rise, for the big trout were otherwise engaged : but, as we all know, the smaller the rise of fish the greater the skill of the angler who can fill his basket. It is not for me to boast. I will not needlessly proclaim what I did under circumstances such as I have foreshadowed. After all, what matters it whether you catch a few trout or many. What angler wants to know any more than he already knows about the kicking, and niggling, and splashing, and dashing of a big trout when you have got him by the lip ?

I will only say about our fishing that we had a most delightful time. The scenery is enchanting ; the meadows are green and yellow ; "the earth is sown with flowers" ; chestnuts in full bloom ; hedgerows white with hawthorn blossom ; birds singing their best songs ; all nature alive, and bright, and gay ; the big trout could be seen in the clear water, floundering about the bottom of deep pools, but rarely casting a look upwards to the feast we set floating above them. The Major may be seen there, sitting on a log, the picture of patience, waiting for a rise, which seldom came ; but when an odd trout here and there bubbled up to the top his deadly betrayer was over him, and he came to grass and to grief.

Amesbury, as you know, is situated in a beauti-

BUTCHER BIRD.

ful vale on the edge of Salisbury Plain, and the attractions of its surroundings are not limited to angling. The willow beds on the river are the haunts of many birds ; there I caught a glimpse of a pair of butcher birds, quite new to me. Our good host told us that he had seen a pair of them surrounded by their young family. On the haw-thorn spikes around their nest were impaled numberless insects—a sort of butcher's shop, where provisions were laid in, with wonderful instinct, for a rainy day. Bewick says it fre-quently preys on young birds, which it seizes by the throat, and after strangling fixes them on a sharp thorn ; it likewise feeds on grasshoppers, beetles, and other insects.

Another curious scene described to us by our observant friend was one which indicates the strategic capacity of ducks. He saw a flock of about twenty of these intelligent birds spread themselves out in a semicircle across the stream. They then commenced to make a tremendous flapping with their wings, their necks stretched out, and swimming rapidly towards the shore. In this way they drove before them shoals of minnows right up to the gravel. Then they had a fine feast—and "the band played!" Was ever such a scene witnessed before ?

> " And last the little minnow-fish,
> Whose chief delight the gravel is."
>
> WM. BROWNE.

D

One day we took a delightful drive for ten miles northwards, skirting the downs on our left, with the valley of the Avon on our right, through the pretty villages of Figeldean, Nether Avon, to Up Avon ; the road on our right lined with elms and beeches, amongst the green leaves of which were gorgeous golden laburnums and rich red and white May blossoms. On our return from Nether Avon we struck across the plain, and had a glorious five miles' drive over the heather till we came to that marvellous mystery of gigantic stones, known the world over as Stonehenge.

I am not going to describe Stonehenge—that has already been done scores of times—or to tell how, why, or when it came to be where it is. I do not, because I cannot ; an immense amount of archæological skill and antiquarian lore has been expended on these marvellous stones, but they have steadily refused to betray the secret of their origin.

Mr. Edgar Barclay has recently published a most interesting and learned volume, under the title of "Stonehenge and its Earthworks." In this volume he has embodied and sifted all that has ever been written on the subject, and has accompanied his studies with many very elaborate diagrams, and those who are interested in this extraordinary work of our stalwart predecessors on this island will find in this volume an exhaustive account of all the theories of all

STONEHENGE (THE TRILITHON).

previous investigators, as well as practical tests
and measurements of his own. His ground plan
of Stonehenge restored shows that the design
consisted of an outer circle of thirty uprights,
supporting twenty-eight traverse stones or lin-
tels ; then there is an inner circle of smaller
uprights, and within those, two horse-shoe forms
of stones. In the inner horse-shoe is an enormous
slab called the Altar.

These giant stones are all that now remain,
but who knows that they were not once covered
over and the interspaces filled in with some
perishable material? If you pay a visit to
Stonehenge on June 21st, and stand on the
south-western side at three o'clock in the morning, and looking between a trilithon of stones
at the back of the Altar Stone, and through
another opening on the opposite side of the
circle, the point of sunrise will be seen over the
tip of what is called the Sun Stone, placed
about 100 feet beyond the outer circle. In front
of this Sun Stone is an enormous stone lying
flat, which is called the Slaughter Stone, on
which the victims were sacrificed. That great
Sun Stone, 16 feet high, and standing alone,
and slightly bending forwards and looking towards the temple, its back to the rising sun,
looked, as we drove across the plain, exactly
like the figure of an enormous Druid priest
or monk. One could almost realize the flow

of a magnificent beard, and the shape of the arms beneath the graceful folds of a long cloak.

Here it was, in this "forest of monoliths grouped upon the grassy expanse of plain," that "Tess of the D'Urbervilles" found a brief refuge from her pursuers. She had flung herself upon an oblong slab that was sheltered from the wind by a pillar—evidently the slab known as the Altar Stone—and there she slept, "till the light grew strong, and a ray shone upon her unconscious form, peering under her eyelids and waking her"; and then they marched her off to her doom.

The net result of all speculative inquiry seems to be that Stonehenge may possibly not be of the vast antiquity by many authorities attributed to it, that it is not as old as the many barrows surrounding it, and that it is not altogether of Druidical origin. The prevailing opinion seems to be that it belongs to the fourth century A.D., and was erected as a memorial of what is called "The *Amesbury Massacre*." About the year A.D. 429, Hengest the Saxon prepared an entertainment, to which he invited the British king, nobles, and officers, to the number of about three hundred. Then, concealing his wicked intention, he ordered three hundred Saxons to conceal each a knife under his foot, and to mix with the Britons, and when they were sufficiently inebriated, he ordered each man to draw his knife and kill his man.

I will only further remark that this extraordinary assemblage of monster rocks could only have been brought together by giants of the olden time, whether by Druids in prehistoric time or by Britons and Romans at a later period; and could hardly have been erected, at such an enormous cost, merely to commemorate such a massacre as this; they must have been erected for some more needful purpose. Stonehenge is truly worthy of a long pilgrimage, if the result be only to excite one's awe and wonder. It is only a pleasant walk of two miles from Amesbury village to this unique and ancient mystery.

Salisbury Plain is prolific in hares—we saw numbers of them in our drive across the plain—and I was glad to note this, and also the great number of skylarks scattered all over the downs, because elsewhere both hares and larks are said to be growing scarce.

I would fain close my rambling notes with a word in recognition of the hospitality of our good friend who found for us this fine opportunity for a spring outing, such as we who are denizens of a great city know how to appreciate.

CHAPTER V.

MAY FLY FISHING ON THE ITCHEN (1896).

FRIDAY, May 22, 1896, was the day on which I had the first intimation that the May Fly was *up*, but this was not a proper use of the word, for on perambulating our bit of the Itchen from one end of our tether to the other, we saw perhaps one May Fly sailing or being blown down stream or clean off the water once in 200 or 300 yards. It seemed useless to fish with the May Fly. The Alder brought me in a good $1\frac{1}{2}$ lb. trout and a brace of grayling, which had to go back.

May 23.—This was a fine, dull day. Wind, north-west. Fish taking every May Fly that came up, but these were only intermittent. I did a fair day's work, and was satisfied.

May 24 (Sunday).—A charming day. Fish taking May Fly in peace and quietness, unterrified by shadow of man or rod or barb-winged imitation.

May 25.—A fine day with strong wind. May Fly intermittent, but all taken. We captured between us five brace of trout besides many grasping grayling, which had to go back for autumn reminders.

May 26.—A similar day, and our taking was similar.

May 27 and 28.—I may say ditto.

May 29 (Friday).—A memorable day—bright, genial, warm. May Fly up on river and meadow in something like the old-fashioned style, but what was most remarkable, was the undoubted fact that trout were not taking them. They would not, and could not, be lured by any imitation of May Fly—or any natural fly that floated—and yet they were greedily disturbing rather than rising above the water. What did it mean? Our theory was that they were gorging themselves with the May Fly larvæ (just when the final ecdysis occurs), snatching each insect before it came to the surface and completely got rid of its grubby shell.

We were four of us, and amongst us at least three as accomplished fly casters as may often be seen together (I say nothing of the fourth, "The A. A."). We tried a variety of May Fly imitations, chief amongst them the G.O.M. We tried Alder, Ginger Quill, Duns of various hues, but I am compelled in truth to say that during the whole of that lovely day, though we toiled like men, hungry and starving, we came home with "a beggarly account of" empty baskets. Not a fish would come at us.

May 30 (Saturday).—My last day for May Fly, 1896. I did fairly well, but the rise seemed almost over, though I hear since that on the three days following there was still a *rise* of May Fly, and that fish were taking the spent fly.

I know that my experience does not go for much amongst anglers, but I have thought it just worth while briefly to record my doings. I should say, on the whole, that it has been about as bad a season for May Fly fishing as we have had for some years. It came on quite ten days earlier than is usual on our water, and seemingly in too straggling and uncertain a way wholly to attract and absorb the attention of our well-fed trout, although it was most noticeable that when a big trout was thoroughly aroused from his lethargy how eagerly he would rush at every fly that came within a roving distance of his lair.

With reference to the May Fly, it had been maintained by a distinguished connoisseur in all matters pertaining to angling, that neither trout nor grayling care a *fico* for the mere colour of your "imitation"—and he suggested for a change that a May Fly dyed *pink* or *deep red* might prove a brilliant attraction for the gay old stagers in our deep pools.

Accordingly I put this theory to a practical test. I put on my collar a May Fly of a brilliant *red* colour. I tried it for an hour or more—placing it as seductively as possible over many a rising fish—and I am bound to say that my experience does not justify me in recommending for general use this singular departure from the more modest colour with which Nature usually paints her May Flies.

You who are accustomed to watch the action of fish in a stream have, of course, noticed that dart-like and diagonal disturbance of the water which a big trout makes when you startle him from the bank on which you may be walking.

Well! No sooner had my red fly come over this rising fish than similar dart-like streaks could be seen in every direction. This fiery demon of a fly was a conspicuous object on the water for many yards around. Not only would my particular trout bolt like a shot, but every other fish in his immediate neighbourhood would make similar tracks!

This, you will please to understand, was a scientific experiment, and from it I am led to conclude that both trout and grayling, and possibly many another kind of fish, can not only distinguish flies by their natural colours, but that of all the seven prismatic colours *red* is that which scares them like the very deuce.

Green Drake and Yellow Drake and Gray Drake they take most kindly to—but I am well assured, from actual experience, that *Pink* or *Red* Drake they cannot and will not stand !

Notwithstanding the fact that our lines were not so frequently tightened nor our baskets so heavy as a genuine May Fly rise leads one to expect, I am bound to say I had a very pleasant week. Our straw-thatched hut at the corner of our water, under the shadow of a lovely hawthorn in full bloom, is truly a pleasant retreat for peaceful rest after the hard work of toiling down to it. There one can sit and watch up stream for rising fish ; there it was that I saw a big banker fifty yards up absorb a May Fly with the slightest motion possible. It was a long and difficult cast up stream against wind and bank, but I came down upon him nicely. He seized my fly promptly, and led me a lively dance for about ten minutes ; but at last he made a dash under a ledge deep under the bank, from which nothing would move him. At length my hold loosened, and he went away in triumph with my fly and a bit of gut fast in his mouth. A few days after, "Piscator Major" wrote to me that he had caught my two-pounder, with my fly and gut still in him, to prove his identity ! I think it quite too bad. That trout might, more happily both for himself and me, have come straight into *my* basket last week—he would have been saved much tickling and worry in his mouth—and I should have been proud of him. Of course I claimed the fly.

CHAPTER VI.

"ANIMALS AT WORK AND PLAY—THEIR ACTIVITIES AND EMOTIONS."[1]

N old friend offered the other day to make me a present of a beautiful Scotch terrier, a pup of the purest breed, whose value in coin of the realm was represented by many sovereigns. I was touched by the offer, and would fain have accepted him, but the reflection was forced upon me, if I do accept him, what can I do with him? I live in a small suburban pill-box on the top of a hill; it is surrounded by a charming flower garden, which is the admiration and, I think, the envy of all my neighbours, and I am proud of it. But the architect, in planning the premises, made no allowance or accommodation for the keep of a dog. There is no back yard or stable yard. It is true I might build for him a little wooden house down at the bottom of the

By C. J. Cornish. London: Seeley and Co., Limited.

garden, and chain him up there. But there are several objections to that plan. In the first place, what is the good of having a dog if he must be always chained up out of your sight? I hate to chain up a dog, to say nothing of the fact that a spirited animal would resent such treatment; he would yelp all day and howl all night; and so perhaps bring about, if not a law-suit, at least a breach of the harmony which should exist between neighbours.

It so happens that we have in the centre of our lawn a lovely bed of begonias—the shiest, the tenderest, the sweetest of all flowers, to my thinking. After much coaxing and tending we have persuaded them to show up their colours above the green leaves. Their lovely tinted, wax-like cupolas are supported on the most brittle stems, and generally the broad, coarse leaves are spread over them to protect them from all winds, just as a hen spreads her wings over her chickens. These lovely little flowers seem as if they were born to blush unseen; but when they do come out, as they are out now in my bed, they are, for richness and delicacy and variety of tints, far beyond all the other flowers in my little *parterre*.

Now you may be quite sure that some day or other that little terrier pup would break loose, and the very first thing he would do would be to make a dash through my bed of begonias—

and one dash would do for them. Geraniums
and fuschias and such like can stand a little
rough usage of a dog-like nature, but the fragile-
stemmed, delicate begonia would be snapped
off at once by swish of tail or tread of foot. The
next thing that dog would do would be to bite
the butcher boy, or the newspaper boy, or the
milkman, and so render me liable to a heavy
fine, and last of all he would dash off like mad
into the street without a muzzle; he would be
taken up by the police, and carried off to the
Dogs' Home. There they would starve him for
a few days, then give him a dose of prussic acid,
and so would end the life of that lively little
terrier pup. No, my dear good friend! I am
truly obliged to you, but I regret that for his
own sake I must not accept your interesting
present!

A young lady friend of mine once had a
beautiful "Pomeranian" spaniel; she loved, nay,
she adored that dog. Truly to look at he was
one of the prettiest creatures that ever was seen.
His long white hair as white as milk and as soft as
silk; his dark, bright, beautiful, intelligent eyes:
his graceful head and his curly tail, made him a
thing to be admired; but that dog was hated
by everyone but his mistress, and the more they
hated the more she adored him. He was deceitful above all dogs, and desperately wicked.
The school children in the streets fled at the

very sight of him. He had his likes and his dis-
likes. To me he was generally civil, at least
he never bit me. His greatest aversion, perhaps,
was the postman, who wouldn't come near the
house till he knew he was locked up. The
parson he didn't like at all, and once tore off
the skirt of his coat. He seized a young lady
by the heel and tore off her slipper. The doctor
he pretended to like, but once suddenly seized
him by the hand and tore the flesh to the
bone. At length things came to such a pitch,
he had bitten so many people, that threats
of actions at law came pouring in, and something had to be done. So he was sent to a
dog dentist, several of his teeth were drawn,
others broken or filed down, and his mistress
mourned for him sorely. At last he came back
home, much humbled, but as deceitful and
vicious as ever. He still did all he could to bite
people and to frighten children. Still his mistress loved him. During her absence from
home for a day or two he died suddenly of
spasms ; and she wept and bemoaned him
bitterly.

Really, Mr. Cornish, I must apologize. The
very title of your book, "Animals at Work and
Play," started me off in the wrong direction. I
meant to have devoted time and space to your
fascinating book ; but it does not much matter.
The very title is enough to attract all lovers of

natural history to the book, and when they have once got it in hand they will not part company with it easily. Besides, I had no thought of writing a critique upon it. I am not a professed naturalist or a professed critic. I am content to take your stories about quadrupeds and bipeds, birds, beasts, and fishes ; to read them and be amused, like other people, and not to question your accuracy about this or that.

It is very amusing to learn how animals make their beds ; how they sleep and make their toilettes ; how they love and how they hate ; how they play, and what a curious sense of humour they often display. It is surely interesting to be told by a patient and quick observer what animals do in rain ; how birds are lost in storms : " Sweating Bees," " Animals in Sickness," " Dangerous Animals in Europe," " Sanctuary of Wild Birds," " The Animal View of Captivity," etc. These are some of the chapter headings. A philosopher made a grand discovery the other day, that human beings, from Adam to this end of the nineteenth century, had been lying abed the wrong way ; instead of sleeping with their heads on their pillows, the proper thing to do, according to him, is to put their feet there and their heads away down where the feet used to be. This way of sleeping is said to be a perfect cure for insomnia and many other ills to which mis-taken humanity has hitherto been subject. Why

THE EUROPEAN BADGER (*Meles taxus*).

in this respect have we not long ago taken a lesson from the badger? Mr. Cornish informs us:

"The badger takes a quantity of grass in to make its bed in the winter, and removes this when he comes out more freely in the spring. But the oddest fancy of the badger in bed is that it *actually sleeps on its head.* This is true in any case of one of the Zoo badgers. Twice when the straw in which he buries himself has been removed, the writer has seen him, not curled upon his side, but with the top of his flat head on the ground, and the rest of his body curled over it, as if it had fallen asleep in the middle of turning head over heels."

This no doubt fully explains the general healthfulness of the badger, and accounts for its longevity. It is probably the only living creature that has preserved this original law of nature. But is there not some trace of it still left in humanity? How is it that human beings in the tadpole stage are so fond of standing on their heads instead of their feet, till the tendency has been smacked out of them? Our philosopher above mentioned had probably discovered the secret of the badger, and from it deduced the new pillow theory as a stage in the right direction.

It would be easy to quote page after page from this interesting book, but that would be unfair to the author. Perhaps the most interesting chapter to anglers is the one on "The Invisible

E

Food of Fishes." It appears that oatmeal given to oysters to fatten them has just the opposite effect, and causes them to lose weight and die, and flour soon poisons them, whilst " the typhoid bacillus is destroyed by passing through the oyster's alimentary canal," which is good news for the owner of oyster beds. What was until recently thought to be the principal food of river fishes now appears to play only a limited part in their maintenance, and the common fisherman's view, that river fishes work hard for their living, and subsist mainly on worms and grubs, with a change to May Fly in the season, and occasional feasts of ground bait and paste, is almost as far removed from fact as the showman's description of the elephant's diet as consisting mainly of cakes.

It seems to have been a problem hitherto unexplained as to what non-carniverous fish, from the whale to the pilchard or herring, could possibly find to live on in seas apparently barren of all kinds of food. The explanation is that :

" The microscopic creatures which are in parts of the Atlantic massed so thickly in the water as to discolour the surface, and give abundant food for the whale, are present, not so thickly, but in numbers comparable to motes in the air, in all parts of the sea. For the purposes of the herring and the pilchard, and countless other shell fish and zoophytes, the upper waters of the sea are in fact a nutritive soup teeming with food exactly suited to their need. These microscopic creatures are the basis of all the larger life of the ocean, and in a great degree of the growth and increase of fresh water fishes. Some of these tiny creatures are water-fleas, others like carpaced shrimps . . . and are of prodigious fecundity. . . . In rivers they are almost the sole food of all young fish, and probably the main resource of the older fish when other supplies fail. In the first days of spring the creatures in every stage—eggs, larvæ, and perfect though microscopic *entomostraca*— swarm in the water, on the mud, and on the foliage of the water plants. At such times even trout feed mainly on them . . . they are then said to be *tailing."*

We all know what *tailing* means from an angler's point of view. Let the day be ever so promising, the wind in the right quarter, and insects abundant on the surface, if a trout is *tailing* you might as well pack up and go home.

"They are eating the weed bare of the cling- ing film of microscopic larvæ, of water-fleas, *cyclops*, and other fresh water *entomostraca*. . . . Experiments made on trout showed that when fed upon worms only they grew slowly; others fed upon minnows did better ; but a single fish fed upon insects weighed twice as much at the end of the experiment as a pair of those reared upon worms and minnows respectively. . . .

Carp were formerly believed to be vegetable feeders, and the carp ponds of Germany used to be drained and planted with rye as carp food. So it was, but only as being itself food for the microscopic millions. The carp chews the water weed, sucks off the insects, and then spits it out again."

There have been many learned discussions in "The Fishing Gazette" as to how salmon manage to live in fresh water without the least particle of food ever being found in their stomachs. Well, here is the solution : They "live upon nothing but victuals and drink," but of the microscopic and invisible kind now known as *entomostraca;* just as whales and pilchards and herrings flourish in seas apparently barren of all food, so do salmon live and flourish on the billions of invisible creatures swarming in rivers, which they assimilate as soon as swallowed, and therefore no food is ever found within them. I regard this theory as a discovery. *Palmam qui meruit ferat,* to Mr. Cornish belongs the palm. I only tell the story.

The mention of carp reminds me that when " Piscator Major " and I were in Paris some time ago, we ran down to Fontainebleau solely and wholly for the purpose of having a look at the big carp, for doth not our master say that he is " the *Queen* of rivers," in the same sense, I suppose, as the salmon is called the *King* of rivers—"a stately, a good, and a very subtle fish." He also says that "if he have water room and good feed, will grow to a very great bigness and length ; I have heard, to be much above a yard long." The fine old château which Napoleon III. renovated, and built a gorgeous theatre therein, was closed when we arrived at five o'clock. The theatre was completed a few weeks only before the outbreak of the Franco-Prussian war of 1870, and so the poor emperor saw it only on a few occasions, and it has never been played in since. The park gates were open, and the fine lake was accessible. There is a tradition floating about that this lake contains carp more than a hundred years old. On the other hand, it is said that the Cossacks, in 1815, drained the lake dry, and ate up every carp. If that is so, and the lake was immediately restocked, the oldest carp to be found there now can barely have reached the respectable age of *eighty*. It is certain, however, that the lake swarms with carp of all ages, and they seem to be in a very lively and healthy condition.

An old woman sits in a small alcove surrounded with loaves of bread, which she sells to the visitors at a penny a hunch. The carp were there in hundreds, and we fed them. Fine fun it was to see the helter-skelter dash they would make for a small lump of bread. A large crust caused most excitement, because they could not

easily seize it, and presently a big old fellow, a
yard long, would sail round or come up from
below, push the others aside with his pig-like
snout, and swallow the lump just as an old sow
would. It was interesting to notice the respect
paid to a pair of stately swans by all the carp—
big and little. When they sailed in for a share
of the food there was a general skedaddle, and
the swans took their bread with proper dignity.
We saw several fellows there that were quite a
yard long ; and a few nearly white, which gave
them the appearance of venerable age. They
seemed to thrive on bread, but probably more
so on the invisible *entomostraca* mentioned by
Mr. Cornish.

It will be seen that I have made of this little
book a sort of peg to hang a variety of odds and
ends upon. I will finish by recommending it
heartily to all readers who can find interest in
the doings of all sorts of animals, when at work
or at play.

CHAPTER VII.

ROUND AND ABOUT LOWESTOFT.

OWESTOFT being situated on the most easterly point of England, and fully exposed to any sea breezes that may blow from the north, or the east, or the south, most certainly possesses at least this one advantage over many of the seaside resorts on the south coast, that its breezes are bracing and its air invigorating ; and, as these happen to be the recuperative qualities most needed by those who go down to the sea, Lowestoft has become very popular, and consequently, it must be added, very dear for the accommodation it affords, as compared with other and more fashionable resorts. The season here is short ; limited, indeed, so I am told, to two or three months, which are the harvest times for the inhabitants, and it is no discredit to them to say that they do their best to make hay while the sun shines.

The expense of board and lodging does not weigh quite so heavily on me as it does on large family parties occupying many rooms ; and weekly family bills, for being braced up by the breezes and strengthened by the sea air which pervades Lowestoft, make a large inroad on holiday expenses, and folk cannot live on breezes alone. Altogether, therefore, I think it may be said to be an expensive place. The people who go there in such crowds seem to be of a class most easily satisfied with the very mildest of entertainments. Bands play at intervals, an open-air concert on the sands in the evening, preaching and disputing and shouting, make up the sum total of what the visitor will at any time encounter in a tramp through the whole extent of south Lowestoft, from the Grand Hotel to the bridge, which separates the north from the south, as well as the inner and the outer harbours. At the north end of north Lowestoft is an exceedingly pretty little park, and down below on the Denes is the model fresh water yacht pond, an interesting and attractive spot, on which young people sail their boats. The largest of these juvenile yachts are modelled to scale on the best racing yachts of the Solent, and miniature races take place periodically under Yacht Club rules.

Two rival phrenologists occupy tents on different parts of the sands, and seem always to be

THE BEACH, LOWESTOFT.

engaged in examining the heads of the rising
generation, and teaching the anxious mothers
how to teach their children to avoid the shoals
and quicksands of life which their bumps fore-
shadow. It would be curious to compare the
opinions of these two learned scientists on their
examination of the same head.

Lowestoft and its surroundings are certainly
not without many attractions. There is a very
long and attractive pier, and there must be two
or three miles or more of walls surrounding the
harbours, and on these walls or platforms may
be seen at any time of the day hundreds upon
hundreds of anglers, young and old, fishing for
anything that may come ; and it is surprising to
see the number of little fishes these persevering
and most patient young and old anglers will pull
out.

Then there are the neighbouring broads and
rivers. One day we went, some of us by rail and
some by steamer, to St. Olave's, which is within
a mile or two of the enchanting Fritton Lake, so
well known to all anglers. There we hired boats
and floated idly round the lake ; or, anchored in
seductive places, we fished and fished, but nothing
came of it but the fun of the thing. Men, women,
and children—our family party a-fishing numbered twelve—all chattering, all fishing, all
swinging rods and lines, and floats, and hooks,
and baits about in the liveliest manner imagin-

able.   A most delightful way of fishing, but to
the surprise of some of us not a fish was caught.
They kept off at a respectful distance from our
boats, and were much amused at the wild antics
being played above them on the surface of the
water; for if they could not hear the laughter,
and shouting, and screaming of the youngsters
over their heads, they could plainly enough see
the fantastic allurements now splashed down
upon them and now as suddenly jerked up.   It
amused the fishes, it amused the children, we
were all amused, and no one was hurt.

When we got ashore again we wandered
through the pretty woods and gardens—we
romped on the lawns, and had swings and
other diversions ; and altogether we had a jolly
time, old ones as merry and light-hearted as the
young ones.   Fritton Lake is over three miles
long and probably a mile wide in some places,
much narrower in others.   It is charmingly
surrounded by dark green woods, with pretty
nooks and corners, where, shutting out the
troubles and sorrows, the worrits and anxieties
of the wicked world we have left behind, we
might long to fish and float on and on for ever.

Another time, on serious angling bent, we left
the children to play on the sands, and started
off, " Piscator Major," another young enthusiast,
and I, for a day's fishing in the Yare.

It is curious to note as you pass along these

rivers and broads the number of ardent anglers you will see patiently sitting in punts moored to the banks and waiting for a bite, and how, quite unconsciously, as it were, they would, if they happened to be successful, haul up their keep nets (which are usually suspended outside the boat in the water), and, as if to see that all was right, pretend to examine their catches, but really to show us passers-by what tremendous fellows they were for catching fish ! Well, we who laughed at their mild ostentation, and envied their success, were bent, when we reached our destination (at Coldham Hall, on the Yare), on doing the same thing.

We hired a punt ; we provided lunch for ourselves and ground-bait for the fishes. We had a couple of long poles, which we stuck in the mud at each end of our punt, and to these, having found a likely place for fishing, we moored ourselves. We were careful not to get too far out in the stream on account of the big steamers and yawls, and yachts and barges that were constantly passing up and down the river. We measured the depth of water, and adjusted our floats and shot and baits thereto, so that the bait might not be suspended midway from the bottom or lie idly thereon—an inch or two off the bottom is best.

Meanwhile we had cast into the water many a handful of ground bait. The bait we used was paste, sometimes white, sometimes coloured pink, always nice and tough so that it would bear rather rough swinging from the rod to get it out a good distance from the punt ; and so we three sat in that punt patiently watching our floats. I may say that we had only two rods between us, for I regarded myself as an outsider—a mere spectator—and I must say that sitting in a punt for hours, watching a float, with a hot sun in front of you and a cold easterly wind blowing lumbago blasts at your back is *not* the kind of fishing that enlists my sympathy ; I soon grew tired of it. But there I was imprisoned, in deep water, ten yards from shore, and to get there meant pulling up our mooring poles and rowing a hundred yards away for a landing place, thus disturbing all the arrangements. Aware of this, I for a long and weary time exercised all the patience at my command, but I at last begged to be put ashore, and I was glad to stretch my stiffened legs by prowling about the fields. I had seen my young friends pull in a number of small fish, and I had caught one or two myself.

There does not seem to me to be much skill required in this sort of fishing—patience is the great thing, and luck has something to do with it, else why did that big bream not come at me instead of the Major ? How that fool of a fish fought and splashed and dashed about was good to see, but the Major had him in a firm grip, and after many a struggle he got him to the top of the water; but we had no landing net, and to have lifted him bodily by the hook and gut into the boat would have been an impossible feat, he would inevitably have smashed that slender gut. Happy thought! We hauled up our keep net, already alive with a number of decent roach. We managed to get this under the monster, and we got him into it, where he made a lively time for himself and the others suspended in the water till the boat came home.

When brought ashore he was pronounced to be the biggest bream that had been caught in those waters this season. Bream are not usually considered to be particularly good for food, but our ferryman, to whom we presented him, said all that depended upon the way he was cooked. "First," says he, "let him be well scraped and cleaned (he had just jumped out of the net and wallowed in the mud), and then"——but I am not called upon to give a lesson in cooking bream, let it be sufficient to say that he seemed delighted to get him, and intended to call his friends and his neighbours together and give them a jolly supper.

"Piscator Major" and the other young enthusiast seemed to be well satisfied with their day's sport. I do not think I care just yet about having another dose of punt fishing, but to those

who like this kind of fishing what unlimited
scope there is on these great broads and rivers
of the east for an unlimited number of anglers !
and seeing that so much of the fishing is free,
and you can hitch up your boat wherever you
please, so long as you do not interrupt the traffic,
one's chief cause for surprise is that so few
London anglers find their way down to them,
notwithstanding the fact, which one would have
thought was pretty well known, that, contrary
to some other railway companies, the G.E.R.
affords every facility, accommodation, and
economy to *bonâ fide* anglers throughout their
system, and the expense of getting down to
these waters is certainly not burdensome, while
the sport for those who like it is pretty certain
and good.

I have not the conceit to suppose that I am
the only one who has ever made a pilgrimage
from Lowestoft to Blunderstone. One day A. M.
and I took a small Norwich car (and very con-
venient little traps they are) and drove over
to Blunderstone—being about five miles from
Lowestoft—to see if by chance we could discover "The Rookery," the house in which David
Copperfield was born, and where his earliest
days were spent. Blunderstone is a long
straggling village. Our driver had never heard
of David Copperfield, nor for a long time could
we find anyone in the village who knew where

the Rookery was (the rooks, it will be remembered, had deserted the elms before David's
time). One woman, standing in her little front
garden, when we politely asked if she could
direct us to the place we were in search of,
would not give us a reply at all ; she rushed
into her house and banged the door behind her.

At length we came to the blacksmith, a good-
tempered, bright-eyed, young fellow, who clearly
had the whole story by heart. We were told to
bear round to the right, and to take the first
turning to the left till we came to a barn, and
there, standing back some two or three hundred
yards from the road, we should see the identical
house which had lately fallen almost into ruins,
the roof off, but had now been thoroughly
repaired. "There," said the blacksmith, "you
will see the window at the back where young
David Copperfield used to lie and watch the
church and churchyard and the daws and rooks
for hours in those doleful times when he was
incarcerated for biting Mr. Murdstone's fist."

We found the barn and the house as directed
--now a freshly painted pleasant villa, with a
parlour to the right and a parlour to the left, the
door in the middle. The house being a considerable distance from the road, with a small
paddock and lawn intervening, we thought it
not rude to stop our steed in the road in order
to have a good look at it ; but we had to move

on, for a man immediately came out with a gun in his hand.

I do not pretend to say, or wish it to be inferred, that that man meant to shoot us—indeed, I am inclined to doubt whether he even saw us ; he was most likely going to shoot at the blackbirds or starlings in the fruit trees in the garden at the back—but we were curiously startled ; it is not comfortable to stand staring at a man with a gun in his own garden, however amiable his real intention may be, and so we drove on, contenting ourselves with a glimpse at the front of the house, not daring to approach it nearer. We also got a glimpse of the very interesting looking old church with its remarkable round tower.

We had only two hours at our disposal when we left Lowestoft, and that time was nearly up, so we had to content ourselves with the glimpses we had got. We travelled for some distance along the Yarmouth road, so familiar to David, and Barkis, and Peggotty, and all the rest of 'em. Surely it was somewhere along this road that Mr. Barkis, the carrier, on learning that Peggotty made all the apple parsties and did all the cooking, instructed David (whom he was taking from his home to Yarmouth), if he should happen to be writing to Peggotty, to add those immortal words, " Barkis is willin'."

CHAPTER VIII.

THE PROSE OF FLY FISHING.

September, 1896.

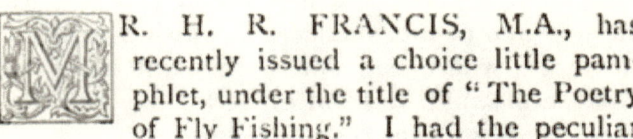

R. H. R. FRANCIS, M.A., has recently issued a choice little pamphlet, under the title of " The Poetry of Fly Fishing." I had the peculiar privilege of reading this charming little work under circumstances not altogether conducive to the pleasure or enjoyment of fly fishing—for I read it one day sitting in our fishing hut, where I had perforce taken shelter from a continuous downpour. My lively little basket carrier comforted me with a contribution to the poetry of fly fishing not to be found in Mr. Francis's book. " Never mind, sir," said he,

> " Sunshine and shower
> Change every half-hour."

Rhyme only partly true in my case, for the sunshine did not appear at all, but the rain

continued all day. It was a happy thought that
led me to put that pretty booklet into my pocket,
for it betrays a personal acquaintance with all
that has been said by all the poets, ancient and
modern, on the subject of angling. It is, indeed,
a sort of defence of the poetry of angling against
maligners who have stated as a proof of defect
that angling has found but little favour with the
poets—and where could be found so suitable a
place for reading it as in a hut specially appro-
priated to anglers, and looking out, as it does,
from beneath the shade of a wide-spreading
hawthorn, where one can sit and watch the big
expanse of water in front of us for any fish that
rise—but none ever rose.

My lively boy, whom I have already quoted,
and who seems to have something of the spirit
of a young naturalist in him, drew my attention
to the performances of three "dabberchicks," as
he called them, swimming about in the pool
regardless of us, perhaps because they could
not see us. At one moment the water would be
quite clear of them—then up they were again,
alternately diving and swimming in a happy
state of enjoyment. "I wish I could dive and
swim like they," cried young twelve-year-old,
"I'd soon put some fish in the basket."

A little further up stream were a pair of birds,
unknown to me, feeding on a small island of cut
weeds that had not long before been released

from one of the arches of the bridge above. A
mixture of decayed vegetable matter, apparently
alive with insects, for the birds seemed to be
delighted with their feast ; now flying up and
snatching insects in the air, now pecking away
at the weeds. "Look up yonder, sir, at that
pair of ' Pollydishwashers ' ; they are such funny
birds, and play such curious antics, specially
when they're flying, popping up and down ; I've
seen lots of 'em about the river."

Then my young naturalist, peering into the
bushes hanging over the water at our feet,
whispered to me to look down there. "See
that water rat on the weeds eating quite con-
tentedly the long stems of grass that come up
from the water ; ain't his eyes bright?" The
little vole was not easily disturbed, and when he
was he would pop into the water for a few
seconds, then up again, and munch away at his
weed as happy as ever.

Presently my young hopeful brought something in his hand. "Look here, sir," says he,
" here 's a case that spiders build their nests in."
A filmy kind of thin bladder, about an inch
in diameter, which had been the birthplace of
hundreds of young spiders. Then my restless
youngster drew my attention to a hawk up in the
sky. " He 's mousing ; you watch and you'll
see him presently put his wings together, and
come flop down like a lump of lead. See,

there he goes. Ah! He 's missed the mouse this time."

This was the way we passed our time, pleasantly enough, in our cosy hut, whilst the rain poured down, and the wind in howling gusts swept the water into rolling waves.

Since I came down to these parts in the May Fly time, which was by no means as good a time as it usually is, I have not had a rod in my hand, and I had chosen a singularly unfortunate time, for the weather was dead against me. I arrived on Friday afternoon, and that evening I caught a fine brace of grayling and a nearly 2 lb. trout, and I have caught nothing since, and my accomplished friend the Professor was equally unlucky. Saturday was an awful day, it rained in torrents all day almost without a break, but we ventured forth well clad in mackintosh and waders. We fished now and then, when we could, in the short intervals, when the heavy rain gave us the least chance, but the wind blew half a gale, and we watched wistfully for a rise. The wind blew all the flies away, and we grumbled because there was no rise.

When the wind fell a little another torrent came on, and we were driven to seek shelter under our favourite wide-spreading ash, which the Professor long since christened " The Pub," a name which it will retain for ever. It must have been in some such way as this that all place names originated ; future generations will therefore please note how and when this doubt-less then celebrated spot came by its odd name. The rain, coming down straighter and heavier than ever, soon found its way through the thick foliage, and we had to move. We made a dash through the pitiless storm for a quarter of a mile, helter-skelter, to our never so pleasant old hut, dripping and draggled like barn-door fowls who couldn't or wouldn't go in when it rained. There we were imprisoned for hours, watching the big bubbles swept away now and then by mighty blasts, rolling and tumbling the usually placid pool into a boiling cauldron. So we started for home at the farm, where we smoked and played chess.

Sunday was wholly given up to Jupiter Pluvius, and Monday was worse than Saturday—we fished all day in the rain without ever even see-ing a rise, for really there was nothing to rise at, and food was plentiful down below.

Tuesday morning was bright but blowy. The Professor, having more chances of choosing his time than I, gave up and went to town. I, as usual, persevered, but still there was no rise, and I got no fish. In the afternoon the rain came down with renewed vigour, and, as already re-corded, I spent my time in the hut till the time came to catch a train for town, and so my little fishing excursion in Hampshire ended.

Friday, Sept. 18, found me on the banks of
the Teme.   A young friend of mine had got me
a day's fishing on a strictly preserved and most
charming stretch of water not many miles above
Tenbury.   It was a lovely day—one might call
it an ideal day for grayling fishing.   My young
friend is an expert ; he had caught over thirty
grayling and trout a fortnight before in the same
water, and his man, who accompanied him,
caught just as many ; he also accompanied us
on this occasion.   We started full of such cer-
tainty of brilliant doings that there was posi-
tively no room for doubt.   In face of these
masters of the angle I, of course, completely
effaced myself.   I felt that I was nowhere.
There was no wind, no rain, and no sun—a dull,
genial, pleasant day.   I was led to expect to see
the pools bubbling with rising fish and the
streams alive with them.   Our man, who on
this occasion was not fishing, except when I now
and then handed him my rod in order that
I might take a lesson in the most approved
method of wet fly fishing with two or three flies
on the cast, to which I had not been used—and
who was loudest in praises of the river, the fish,
and the weather—began soon to wonder what
was the matter.

"What a strange thing it is," said he, "the
fish don't seem to be rising at all ; but never
mind, it doesn't much matter ; they'll take all the

better as we draw the flies gently just under the water." Of course we all practised this method, but it didn't seem to answer—not a fish came near either of us. "All right," exclaimed our enthusiast, "you'll get plenty in the streams and pools lower down." And I am bound to say that I fished—we all fished—our mile or two of water conscientiously, methodically, I may almost say scientifically. I boast not of my own skill, but my friends, both master and man, are undoubtedly born artists, and knew every turn and twist of the river, and where all the best fish are to be found, and yet, after working from 11 a.m. to 5 p.m., we did not catch—we did not see even—a single takable fish. We caught a few samlets, which we put back, and we returned home sorely discouraged, and with baskets as empty as when we set out.

> "Well! I think it is time to put up!
> For it does not agree with my notions,
>   Wrist, elbow, and chine,
>   Stiff from throwing the line,
> To take nothing at last by my motions."
>
> HOOD.

Little bright-eyed, laughing Mary met us at the door with a big dish in her hands, and there were two other young ladies behind her, each one with mocking smiles on her lips, also holding big dishes, hoping, but fearing they were not large enough to hold the contents of our bulging baskets. And didn't they compel us to eat very humble pie. Expecting trout and grayling, they said there was nothing else for dinner but this humble pie, and so we must feed upon that. And, after all, very nice apple pie it was.

Saturday, the 19th, I found myself with my old friends on the banks of the Wye, not very many miles north of Hereford. Here I had had fresh fishing gear sent to me, in the hope of catching a few perch, if not a trout or two ; but I found the river very high and very muddy, and I never unpacked my tackle.

By way of passing the time, on Monday I accompanied my friend on a twenty-five miles' drive through a lovely bit of country. It was a fine, crisp morning, and we reached our destination rejoicing that fine, frosty weather had set in at last. But, alas, no ! Just as we had finished lunch a small black cloud, the size of a man's hand, came up over the hills, and quickly spread itself like a grim pall over the blue heavens, and the rain came pelting down. The first half of our journey was all sunshine, the second half was a deluge. Our good mare brought us home in fine style through the pelting storm. She had trotted fifty miles that day, and was fresh and ready for another fifty next day ; but so were not we. We were diluvians dragged up from the flood to our pleasant Pisgah, which looks down upon the mighty river, now risen by ten feet since we left it in the morning, and still is rising rapidly.

Our road to the station will soon be six feet under water. I rather like it, and won't hurry home. Mushrooms are very plentiful; we have enough to live on if this place should become an inaccessible island.

As Mr. Francis fully justified in his little pamphlet the title he had chosen, "The Poetry of Fly Fishing," so I think I may well claim my experiences on this outing as "The Prose of Fly Fishing."

CHAPTER IX.

A BIBLIOGRAPHY OF GILBERT WHITE.[1]

OME years ago I made a brief pilgrimage to the village of Selborne, celebrated the world over as the birthplace and deathplace of Gilbert White. It was in the month of April; a bright, sunny time, when all nature was gay and smiling.

Selborne, as White describes it, lies in the extreme eastern corner of the county of Hampshire, bordering on the county of Sussex, and not far from the county of Surrey—is about fifty miles south-west from London. On the south-west is a vast hill rising three hundred feet above the village, which consists of one straggling street about three-quarters of a mile long. The hill overhanging the village is very appropriately named " The Hanger." The whole of the hill facing it is covered with beech trees, " the most

[1] "A Bibliography of Gilbert White, the Natural Historian and Antiquarian of Selborne." By Edward A. Martin, F.G.S. (The Roxburgh Press.)

lovely of all forest trees, whether we consider its smooth rind or bark, its glossy foliage, or graceful pendulous boughs."

The house in which Gilbert White was born, and in which he died, is called "The Wakes"— a charming old-fashioned house in the village street. This house is, of course, the goal of all pilgrims, who travel to it from all parts, and who, naturally, must be a source of considerable exercise of patience to the occupiers. The house was occupied for many years by Professor Bell, the well-known writer of works on natural history. He dwelt there from 1842 till the time of his death in 1880. Then it came into the possession of General Parr, who left it in 1892. That was the time of our visit to Selborne, and the house was then in a transition state in preparation for the new occupier, and we were not permitted to have even a glimpse of the interior. It has now changed hands again, having been purchased by Mr. Paxton Parkin.

At the time of our visit the older part was in much the same state as it was when Gilbert White died, as Professor Bell seems "to have exhibited the greatest care in retaining, as far as possible, the antique appearance of the house." A northern wing had, however, been added. It would, indeed, be a great pity if such a picturesque old place should be subjected to any "modern improvements."

Although we were unable to view the interior, we got a distant view of the very pleasant lawn and lovely meadow at the back from the footpath which leads up to "The Hanger." The green meadow runs back to the hill, and its whole extent is literally overhung by the lovely beeches.

We had a pleasant walk up the zigzag, through the beeches, and on to the common which runs along the top, and we made many other delightful excursions in the neighbourhood. "The Well Head" is one of the sources of the River Wey—so frequently mentioned by Gilbert White, and of which he gives the following very interesting account :

" At each end of the village, which runs from south-east to north-west, arises a small rivulet. That at the north-west end frequently fails ; but the other is a fine perennial spring, little influenced by drought or wet seasons, called 'Well Head.' This breaks out of some high grounds adjoining to Nore Hill, a noble chalk promontory, remarkable for sending forth two streams into two different seas. The one to the south becomes a branch of the Arun, running to Arundel, and so falling into the Bristol Channel ; the other to the north. The Selborne stream makes one branch of the Wey, and meeting Blackdown stream at Hedleigh, and the Alton and Farnham stream at Tilford Bridge, swells into a considerable river, navigable at Godalming, from whence it passes to Guildford, and so into the Thames at Weybridge ; and then at the Nore into the German Ocean."

The title of Mr. Martin's book strikes me as being a misnomer, erring certainly on the side of modesty, for although it contains three chapters devoted to a most interesting and exhaustive account of all the editions that have ever been printed of "The Natural History and Antiquities of Selborne," together with a chronological summary, showing the date, publisher, printer, editor, number of pages, illustrations, artists, and engravers of every edition ranging from 1789 to 1895 ; it contains beside five other chapters, which supply an admirable, sympathetic, warm-hearted biography of Gilbert White himself, and a charming story of rambles round, and description of, the village of Selborne. The chapters on Gilbert White as a naturalist and as a poet are very pleasant reading.

All admirers of Gilbert White naturally would like to know something of his personal appearance, but, although he often talked about having his portrait painted, it was never done. On this point Mr. Martin says :

"We must imagine White as he rambled along the Lythe, or followed the scent-laden path to the Priory Farm, dressed in the old-fashioned costume of the period. Perhaps he wore a clerical wig, whilst knee breeches and buckles were almost a necessity to a man of his position.   Many years ago an old woman was asked what she remembered of Gilbert White. Her recollection was of a man who used to walk about the hollow lanes 'tap-tapping with his cane.' . . . One account of our author describes him as a little man, perhaps about 5 feet 3 inches n height, and that he often rode a pony. . . . Frank Buckland records that a villager, when asked concerning Gilbert White, replied that ' He was thought little of till he was dead and gone, after which he was thought a great deal of.'   Another villager described him as ' A little, thin, prim, upright man.' "

James Russell Lowell said of Gilbert White's book, that " In simplicity of taste and natural refinement it reminds one of Walton, and in tenderness, of Cowper."

No angler's library would be complete without Izaak Walton and Gilbert White side by side, and the volume to which I am now drawing attention should always be near them.   The popularity of these two delightful writers may be gauged by the number of editions through which their books have gone, and it would not be easy to say which of the two has been the most beloved by the generations which have passed away since these bright examples of humanity and students of nature put on immortality.   In the two hundred years which have come and gone since Izaak Walton died, in 1683, at the age of ninety, *one hundred editions* of "The Compleat Angler" have been called for, the bicentenary of his death (not far from being the tercentenary of his birth) being commemorated by the splendidly produced *one hundredth edition*, edited by Mr. R. B. Marston, who, like Mr. Martin, furnishes a summary with dates of all the editions which precede his edition. This *one hundredth edition* was published in 1888, and it may be said that several very beautiful editions have been published since.

During the century which has elapsed since Gilbert White died, at the age of seventy-three, in the year 1793 (just two hundred years after the birth of Walton), Mr. Martin supplies a list of *fifty-nine editions* of "The Natural History of Selborne." One may reasonably judge from these curious facts that these two delightful writers, and most excellent characters, have had, and will continue to hold, an equal share in the affection of all good people.

CHAPTER X.

"THE COMPLEAT ANGLER." [1]

F making editions of Izaak Walton's "Compleat Angler," it seems likely enough there will be no end, seeing that as time progresses the number increases, and this has been going on for nearly *two hundred and fifty years.*

As already mentioned Mr. R. B. Marston brought out the "Lea and Dove" edition, *being the one hundredth edition.* This was in 1888, and already, only eight or nine years after that date, Mr. Le Gallienne in his introduction to the present edition says : "With the year 1653 came the charming classic, which in the present volume is published for the *one hundred and twenty-first time."*

[1] "The Compleat Angler." By Izaak Walton and Charles Cotton. Edited, with an Introduction, by Richard Le Gallienne. Illustrated by Edmund H. New. Quarto, cloth extra, pp. lxxxiv, 466. London and New York ; John Lane, The Bodley Head. MDCCCXCVII.

Thus *twenty editions* of a work by an author who has been dead two hundred and fourteen years, have been called for during the last eight years. Perhaps the expression "called for" is not quite accurate. The public do not usually call for such editions ; it is rather the enterprise of publishers, who, by producing something attractive and new, *create* a demand, which, but for them, would not have been thought of. Many of the editions enumerated are mere reprints, and the continued demand for such editions is, of course, a true indication of the vitality of the charming old book ; but a newly edited and elaborately illustrated edition, such as the "Lea and Dove" edition, in two quarto volumes, may be said to mark an epoch in the passing time.

The same may be said of the present edition, which is most pleasantly edited, with an intro-duction, by Richard Le Gallienne, and very quaintly and prettily illustrated by Edmund H. New, and, it may be added, printed and bound with the good taste which is a noted charac-teristic of the productions emanating from "The Bodley Head." Such editions as these commend themselves and command the attention of all anglers.

"Perhaps," says Mr. Le Gallienne, "no Eng-lish book except 'The Pilgrim's Progress' and 'Robinson Crusoe,' has been so beloved. Genera-tion after generation has brought to it its young affections, and there seems every reason to suppose that the average of something like a new edition for every two and a half years, which so far the 'Compleat Angler' has maintained, will even be surpassed in the future." In point of immortality—or, perhaps, one should say perpetuation of vitality as well as similarity in simplicity of character of the two writers, Mr. Le Gallienne might have instanced Gilbert White, who, in point of time, is a hundred years younger than Izaak Walton—and whose " Natural History and Antiquities of Selborne" has gone through fifty-nine editions at least, probably many more. These are the kind of books that publishers revel in—there is no author to pay, no one's copyright to infringe, and a certain market for any decently got up edition. Being but an *amateur angler* myself I do not presume to assert the value to modern anglers of Izaak Walton's teachings, but I am inclined to think that Mr. Le Gallienne very considerably undervalues his merits as a practical angler when he says :

"For after all, Walton is a sentiment, at least as an angler ; for I understand that the ordinary Philistine angler, to whom all that pretty warbling talk of birds and honeysuckle hedges has no appeal in comparison with a creel full of speckled trout, thinks but small beer of poor Izaak's angling methods. It is probably among those who have never cast a line (like the present editor), or like Washington Irving have but fished 'to satisfy the sentiment' that the majority of Waltonians are to be found."

Doubtless there are many unsentimental anglers who eschew "the sentiment" altogether, but who, nevertheless, avail themselves of the methods and laws for catching fish which "poor Izaak" has laid down for them.

Undoubtedly Izaak Walton loved nature much, but certainly he loved fishing more, and it is, perhaps, the charming simplicity with which he describes all nature, combined with the accurate knowledge which he displays about all fresh water fish and the various ways of catching them, that keep his memory green in the hearts of all anglers, whether of the sentimental or the " Philistine " class.

I can, however, fully endorse Mr. Le Gallienne's view of the sentimental part of angling :

" One might as well consult a fifteenth century pharmacopœia on Russian influenza as consult 'Honest Izaac' on any of the higher branches of his art. But who minds that? Angling was simply an excuse for Walton's artless garrulity, a peg on which to hang his ever fragrant discourse of stream and meadow. He followed angling, as, indeed, any such sport is most intelligently followed, as a pretext for a day or two in the fields, not so much to fill his basket

as to refresh his spirit, and store his memory
with the sweetness of country sights and sounds.
The angler who merely angles for the sake of
what he can catch is not so much an angler as a
fishmonger."

As regards the facts of Izaak Walton's life, it
was hardly to be expected that Mr. Le Gallienne
could produce anything new—for these he has
relied on former editors. The vexed question
as to whether Izaak Walton was a hosier or an
ironmonger he just leaves where he found it.
His chapter on "Walton's Literary Life and
Friendships" is very interesting, and it closes
with these delightful words : "But it is in vain
we strive by critical reagents to analyze the
unfading charm of this old book ; is it not
simply that the soul of a good man still breathes
through its pages like lavender?"

The text from which this edition is printed
is the fifth edition (the last to receive Walton's
own revision), the spelling being modernized,
including also Part II., by Cotton, respecting
which Mr. Le Gallienne says : "Whatever the
literary skill with which the style of Walton is
imitated, not to say parodied, whatever its
illustrative and associative value, or its import-
ance as a contribution to the art and science of
fly fishing, is, nevertheless, printed as an integral
part of that charming classic, an impertinence.
Its proper place is an appendix, whither I should

have relegated it in this edition had not tradition been too strong to be gainsaid. Whom fame has joined together let no man put asunder."

From a purely literary standpoint, Mr. Le Gallienne is right in his judgment, for there can be no comparison between the genuine simplicity of Walton's writing and the imitative and ostentatious simplicity of Cotton's ; but I am very glad that Mr. Le Gallienne did not relegate Cotton to an appendix, for I am sure it would have condemned his beautiful volume in the eyes of most anglers.

If, as Mr. Le Gallienne says, Cotton "is entirely remembered to-day by his association with Walton," it is pleasant also to remember that but for him we should have known little or nothing about Walton's visits to Beresford Hall, his angling in "The Dove," and the delightful old "Fishing House."

Mr. Le Gallienne dedicates his volume to the Right Honourable Offley Ashburton, Earl of Crewe, in a very pleasant poem of thirteen lines.

As regards the illustrations, which are not the least attractive feature in this memorable edition, they have been made "as thoroughly as possible from a topographical point of view"; mostly made on the spot, comprising views on the districts described by Walton on the Lea from Tottenham to Ware, and by Cotton from Brailsford to Beresford Hall on the Dove. They are very numerous, and of a singular quaintness, pleasing alike to the eye and one's sense of appropriateness. Altogether, they number over two hundred.

We have all heard of the old clock, which makes no other claim to have been Izaak Walton's than that it bears somewhere on it the initials I. W. Mr. New, however, seems to have made a real discovery which I fancy has not been noted before. It is called Izaak Walton's Marriage Chest, and is in the possession of the Right Hon. the Earl of Warwick. The inscription runs as follows :

> "*Izaak Walton.*   *Rachel Floud.*
> Joyned Together In Ye Holie Bonde of Wedlocke
> On Ye 27th Daie of Decembre   A. 1626 D.
>
> > We once were two, we two made one ;
> > We no more two, through Life be one."

Probably this is the Trunk of Linen which in his will he gives to his son, Izaak Walton.

With reference to the Walton Wedding Chest Mr. New sends us the following account. He says :

" The finding of Walton's Marriage Chest was an accident. A cousin of mine was sketching some time ago at Warwick Castle, and the housekeeper took her over the private rooms to see the old furniture, pictures, etc. The chest

IZAAK WALTON'S MARRIAGE CHEST.

stood in a rather dark passage, but she happened to catch the name of Walton on it as she passed, and, knowing I was illustrating 'The Compleat Angler,' she told me of it. Last autumn I wrote to Lord Warwick asking for permission to see the chest, and make a drawing of it if it seemed really genuine. He replied that he was unaware that he had such a chest, but that I was quite at liberty to draw it if I could find it."

Mr. John Lane may well be congratulated in having produced the last of the one hundred and twenty-one editions published up to the present time, and certainly, whether regarded from the editorial or artistic point of view, one of the most remarkable and valuable of all the editions yet published.

CHAPTER XI.

OUR MAY FLY OUTING ON THE TEST.

ATURDAY, May 29, 1897.—I am sitting in a large fisherman's hut on the banks of the Test. The wind is howling overhead, and the waves on the river are like the waves of the sea when the wind is blowing half a gale. This is our second day. Yesterday the sky was leaden and lowering, with occasional glimpses of sunshine. A fair wind was blowing up from the south-west. The May Fly came up occasionally and was promptly taken down, a signal for us to place our imitation on the spot where the real one had disappeared.

Just now, however, I am more interested in the antics of a pair of wagtails—the most elegant and graceful of birds. They are trying all they know to make me believe they haven't got a nest and young ones in the thatch overhead. I know where it is. The hen, dressed in more

sombre garb than her gay husband, peering
through the window, has got sight of me, sitting
in the farthest corner. She has a white grub in
her mouth ; but, instead of flying up to her nest
just above, she is off round the opposite corner,
and so gets to her young by a roundabout way,
and thinks she has tricked me nicely. Now
they are down on the grass yonder, twittering
and digging away, pretending to be quite unconscious that I am watching them. They
think this hut is their property—that it grew up
where it is, quite away in an open meadow, far
away from the habitations of men folk, solely
and specially for them to build their nests in.

Yonder comes the male bird, with a great
bunch of grubs in his mouth, but scolding all
the same. His little bright eye is a Röntgen
ray ; he can see me as clearly as if there were
no glass between us, and I was not sitting
quietly in the darkest corner. Now comes his
wife with another mouthful ; and so they keep
on hour after hour, cramming the maws of those
little monsters up in the thatch. All my readers,
of course, know that the wagtail is the smallest
bird that walks. They may not all know the
riddle propounded, I think, by the late Lord
Melbourne on a solemn occasion:

> " My first is a bird that hops,
> My second makes hay crops,
> My whole we eat with mutton chops."

But I must to business. There is a slight lull of the wind, so I will go down and have another try at that big trout just below the May bush. I pricked him this morning, but I think he must have forgotten that. Yes; there he is—a real beauty, over 2 lb. In this aristocratic stream no fish is takable under 1 lb. The wind is still howling in the trees; my fish is just under the bank on my side. I must get a good way below him and cast up. At my first cast, in a slight lull, I got my fly just above him, and just after he had swallowed a delicious morsel. I had put on a new fly—a favourite, called the G.O.M., specially for him. Up he came, seized it; I struck. He was bewildered, first at the peculiar flavour of this new thing, and then at the strange pricking in his lip. Then he dashed madly across the stream. I held on to him for a long time, but he got down into the weeds, and, alas! I failed to release him, or, perhaps it is more proper to say, I did release him. My hook came away, and I left him behind. There he is still for some more cunning hand. I have lost my last chance at him.

I returned philosophically to the hut, and, while I am waiting here for the wind to moderate its fury, I may as well report our doings of yesterday. We arrived here, no matter where, on the Test on Thursday night, and we started fishing early on Friday morning. A very jolly, bright-eyed keeper, who has met with many curious adventures in his day, attended the Major. He will be easily recognized by a smashed thumb, by which he was pinned between the upper and nether beams of a sluice for four hours in mortal agony. Lenny, a smart young under-keeper, attended me. He has a remarkably quick eye for a rising fish. I may go a little further, by way of identifying our water, by saying that it is without doubt the finest stretch of trout water in the United Kingdom. It has two large carriers, one on each side of the main stream. The latter flows majestically, deep and strong and straight, for about a mile. We had, in fact, both sides of three full rivers to fish.

About this first day's fishing I will only say that we broke the record this season up to date. Our joint efforts produced 19 lb. weight, of which two trout weighed 6 lb., and not one of the rest was under 2 lb. I hooked, and, alas ! I lost in weeds or banks, or through defective gut, six good fish, and the Major lost more from the same causes ; but then he caught more to make up for it. We also caught many grayling, which, of course, at this season, do not count. At the conclusion I could only claim as my share one brace and a half, weighing 6 lb., out of the 19 lb. recorded.

Saturday, 29th, was, as I have already intimated, a tempestuous day. We started early.

I caught, at my first cast over a rising fish, a very fine trout, which I claimed as being up to the standard of 1 lb., but which my *infidus Achates* vowed was only ¾ lb.—it was his opinion against mine, for we had no scales. While we were disputing the fish was dying ; so to settle the question, back he went to his native element, more dead than alive ; he soon recovered his usual health and was off merrily.

The Major caught two or three big ones during the morning, but, as I started by saying, the wind was doing its utmost to drive the big stream back to its source. I did nothing more till lunch came down, and there in the hut we whiled away two or three hours, the wind whistling above and around us.

The long stretch of river I have already mentioned is called the Lake, and up this lake the wind was driving, for the whole stretch is quite unprotected by tree or shrub. The Major started up one side, and I took the other, there being from forty yards to sixty yards of river between us. Not a fly could be seen on the tumbling billows, and there was no sign of a rise.

"Look out !" cried Lenny. "There's a rise up yonder, just about the middle of the stream, by that weed." I had seen the rise at the same time as Lenny. I made a cast, and the wind carried my fly many feet to the left. But cast number three came down nicely just over the

right spot, and whiz! away went my fly up
stream, down, across, and back, and a dash into
the bank close to us. I kept a tight hold all the
time. Now he had got a yard into the bank, and
for a long time would not be dislodged; but
Lenny, by stamping hard on the soft mould—for
he was not more than a foot or two from the
surface—started him out. Off he goes again
down stream, and I could scarcely get ahead of
him. Again he manages to get into the bank,
and again had to be stamped out; but he was
there long enough to get fresh breath and vigour,
and off he made for a bed of weeds. I continued
to pull as hard as I dared to bring him in, but
he got down in spite of my efforts, and there he
stuck, fixed and immovable; not an inch would
he move. My rod was like a rainbow all the
time. At last Lenny, full of excitement, rushed
off across the meadow, quite a quarter of a mile,
to get a long pole; the Major and the keeper on
the other side were also excited. The keeper
urged the Major to wade across, and he started
to come, but his waders only covered his knees,
and my trout was in water six feet deep, so I
ordered him on no account to make the rash
attempt.

Now comes Lenny wildly and breathlessly
running with a long pole on his shoulder. All
was well still; hook and gut, and line and
rod, and arm and angler firmly and immovably

fixed. I feared for my lovely little split cane rod, one of the best and truest ever made by Leonard, of New York. Lenny prodded away at the weeds ; the rod perceptibly straightened. I slackened a bit, and away he goes again down stream, but, failing to reach another bunch of weeds, he tried another dodge. He leapt two feet clean into the air, and then he gave up the fight and came quietly into the net. Altogether he must have given me about twenty minutes of pleasurable excitement. During the process the Major and the keeper were shouting all sorts of advice, to which I paid no heed ; and afterwards they said you should have done this and you should have done that ; but I don't believe that the Major himself, expert as he is, could have handled that plucky trout better than did " The A. A." They clapped their hands and cheered when they saw my fish come to basket. After all he weighed only $2\frac{1}{2}$ lb. The Major caught several bigger ones, but not one that fought like mine.

In connection with this pugnacious fish, I wish to add the following :

NOTICE.—Found, firmly fixed in the root of the pectoral fin of a $2\frac{1}{2}$ lb. trout, a well-made May Fly, pronounced by the Major, from its special style, to be one of Mr. Yarde's " Professors " made by Miss Ellis, of Exmouth. The owner may have it on producing proof of identification. The trout is no longer in evidence, having been eaten the next morning.

In spite of wind and weather, we found, when we came to weigh-in, that we had got exactly he same weight as yesterday—viz., 19 lb.

And now we have to quit this noble river, the finest trout stream I have ever seen, and must be off for " fresh woods and pastures new."

I find I have said little or nothing about the May Fly, but of course it is understood we are fishing with a variety of imitations of that remarkable insect. They were up, it is true, but only fitfully. On Friday they rode placidly on the surface of the water, like frigates of the olden time, or graceful yachts of the Solent ; but on Saturday they were like storm-tossed ships in a wild hurricane at sea, blown hither and thither, and sometimes off the water—there was no chance for the brief life which nature at best allows them. There were more strong-winged swifts about than May Flies ; so that between swift and trout, wind and wave, there were surely none alive of Saturday's brood to tell next day of their rough reception in their new and winged world. So eager and voracious were the swifts that they dashed at our imitations, and three came to grief in this way. One caught my fly and came fluttering down with the barbed destroyer fixed in his bleeding mouth. I released him gently, put him on the grass to test the truth

of the saying that swifts cannot rise from the
ground owing to the length of their wings.   The
saying is proved to be a fallacy.   My swift, after
one or two awkward struggles, sprang into the
air and went his way rejoicing.   The Major
caught another in the same way, and a third
came to grief by dashing against his rod.

"The A. A." and the Major have only now to
express their thanks to the good friend who
afforded them the opportunity of disporting
themselves so delightfully on his beautiful water.

MONDAY, May 31, to Whit Monday, June 7, 1897.—I have not much to record in continuation of our work on the Test, as already described. Owing to my hard work there, I was personally *hors de combat* for four days out of the eight at my disposal. In that wretched period, when the weather was all that could be desired, I was only able painfully to hobble down to our bridge, and there get distant glimpses of the rising trout, and the Major's doings amongst them ; when I say the " Major," be it well understood that " Piscator Major " is meant, for there is another real major fishing over yonder. (I have always used the term *Major* in contradistinction to the *minor* qualifications of " The A. A.") There are plenty of fish here ; indeed, we complain of there being too many grayling, but they are thoroughly well

H

educated, and require much tact in handling, being very well able to distinguish between the *real* and the *imitation*, unless the latter comes before them in a very unquestionable shape.

I am not going to crack up this water as being superior to any other, but I must say that just now the scenery hereabouts is superb, not for grandeur, but for quiet rural beauty. Seated as I am just now in our fishing hut, under the grateful shade of a large May tree, now white with bloom, and looking down upon the placid lake-like stream where the Major last night had an exciting battle with the monarch of the stream, I feel content. The meadow in front of us is one large field of burnished gold, and it is surrounded by woods of various tints of green, mixed also with bits of brown, for the foliage of the young oaks in the woods has been blighted, the leaves curled up and brown, more like winter's remnant than spring's effulgence. Otherwise the foliage is rich and abundant.

The birds hereabouts are more jubilant than they are in common years, and in the bright sunshine all nature is dancing for joy ; but of all the birds of the air there are none happier or more joyful just now than yonder loving couple, yclept Sir Thomas Titmouse and his spouse, Lady Titmouse. Their castle is made of cast iron, quite impregnable ; wise Sir Thomas for choosing so strong a fortress ; but, foolish Sir

Thomas, why did you not consider that you had chosen your abode on a bridge?

When I first made your acquaintance you had the fullest confidence in the goodness of the wingless, featherless bipeds always crossing and re-crossing your bridge. In the iron upright stanchion, forming the end of the bridge, a circular hole, not required for continuation of the lateral bar, had been left, and in that hole you had built your nest. I admired your taste, but I trembled for your future ; your boldness and indiscretion distressed me. Within a yard of where I was leaning on the bridge you and her ladyship flitted in and out of that hole, your mouths crammed with insects, the livelong day. I moved away, and two lazy tramps came and lolled on the bridge ; they soon caught sight of your aperture ; one of them watched you going in, and put his hand over the hole, and shouted as if he had done something wonderful ; I begged him to leave the little birds alone, and presently they both loafed away.

Next morning my tits were at work as busily as ever, but care, and doubt, and suspicion had taken the place of the light-hearted gaiety of yesterday ; now they approached their nest stealthily, and with fear, looking all round to see if any two-legged animal was about. The next morning, when I went down, I found that the boy tending cows in the next field had discovered the nest; he and the other boys had found pleasure in tormenting them, and the next day they had quite disappeared. The young scamps had dropped stones into the pillar, and so no doubt killed the fledglings, and the bereaved parents have experienced the mercilessness and cruelty of boys.

The crop of May Fly is just now proving itself to be far above the average; the air, the bushes, the long grass are clamorous with these noiseless insects; their songs as they dance in the air are too ethereal for mortal ears to hear. Among the deadly enemies of the May Fly I have observed are fish, ducks, geese, swifts, swallows, starlings, dragon flies, and all kinds of birds. It was only to-day that I discovered a new and formidable enemy. Walking through some long and strong weeds, I observed ropes of gossamer suspended from one thistle to another, row above row, and on these lines were suspended like chickens at a poulterer's, as closely packed as possible, hundreds of May Flies. It must have been a happy time for spiders as well as anglers when the cry went forth, "The May Fly is up!" What on earth Master Spider thinks he is going to do with the immense store he has laid up, goodness knows! He is like us anglers on a Saturday night with a stock of fish we know not what to do with. He cannot eat them all himself, and his stock is frail and perishable.

Usually "Piscator Major" takes his fishing very calmly, but now he has come up from the river in a state of considerable excitement. It is about that monarch of the stream I mentioned just now. Sitting on the bench in front of the wooden mansion "sacred to fishermen," he had seen that fish come up with a splash that frightened the calves on the opposite bank, and sent them off galloping across the meadow with their tails up.

There he sat for an hour watching and waiting for another rise ; at length he was rewarded : up he came again. He placed his G.O.M. nicely over him. Then that mild lake became a tempestuous sea ; the lashings of that trout left a track behind like that of a screw steamer ; and so the fight went on for a quarter of an hour. At last he arrived at the point of the net, when he decided to make one other and final effort for liberty ; and, alas ! he went away rejoicing with two yards of collar dangling after him. The gut had given way just in its thickest, and therefore supposed to be its strongest part.

The Major had once caught a five-pounder in the Test, and when this fellow had come within a foot of the net his imagination had already stuffed him and placed him in a glass case as a rival and companion to that Test five-pounder which now hangs in his hall ; and now he has lost him ! A thing to mourn over till next October.

My own exploits on this expedition, and those of the good Professor, who I omitted to say is with us, seem in comparison with this great battle to be but small, and yet, in fact, we did very well. We had many good fights, and often we came off conquerors. Needless for me to go into details, for generally the catching of one trout is very much like catching another trout. The difference between us is that the Major has a forceful way, which *compels* the attention of the trout, who *has* to take what he puts before him. We, the Professor and I, always try gentler and more persuasive measures ; but it does not answer as well—he catches six for every one of ours.

Altogether I may sum up by saying that we have had a very successful and pleasant outing ; glorious weather all the week. On Whit Monday night I caught my last trout in a thunderstorm, and returned to London the same evening, leaving the Professor a few trout still to catch ; I wish him all the success his ardour and quiet skill entitle him to.

The May Fly fishing in these parts may now be said to be over, and altogether I should say that it has been a good season.

CHAPTER XIII.

BANK HOLIDAY FISHING.

August, 1897.

A Singular and Curious Incident.

ISHING on the August Bank Holiday is somewhat of a delusion. A south-easterly wind, a blazing sun, and water of the transparency of gin do not seem to be conducive to a rise of flies or a rise of trout and grayling. Yet it need hardly be said that, even under these conditions, it is better to come face to face with Nature and be baked, than to sit in a London office and be stewed. We had two days of it—Saturday and Monday. We could not catch fish in the sun, first, because we could not stand the heat ; and, secondly, because there were no fish to catch. We traversed the whole length of our water from above the bridge to the fishing hut without seeing a rise. Trout and grayling alike had

buried themselves in the weeds or hidden in the banks. We walked, or, I may say, we loafed, down the river, lingering under every bit of available shelter till we reached our *dulce domum, piscatoribus sacrum.*

There, as always, we found a cool and calm retreat under the friendly shade of our beautiful May tree, backed up by an equally friendly wide-spreading oak, and surrounded by a colony of hazel nut trees.

There we sat in our easy chairs, and lunched, and chatted, and read ourselves to sleep, and so we passed the livelong day. Sometimes we amused ourselves by watching the antics of that bold young vole whose acquaintance I had made last year, who, regardless of our presence, would jump out of his hole in the bank, almost under our feet, on to a tuft of drift weeds, and search about for the particular succulent stems that suited his taste. Of these he would gather a full mouthful, and drag them up to his hole ; munch away at them for a time, and then another plunge for more. This little game he seemed to be keeping up all day.

It was not on either day till after six o'clock, when the sun was beginning to climb down behind the western hills, that the fish made any motion whatever ; then here and there the small grayling, amid stream, began to make ripples on the smooth surface of the water, and later on a larger circle would be seen, and so by degrees, and for a short time, certain portions of the river, where the big grayling occasionally flopped up, gave some sign that it was not destitute of fish ; but they rose fitfully, and it was not possible to see what they were rising at, for there was no fly visible.

I caught a couple of brace of grayling the first evening with the Red Tag—a delusive deception, like no insect that ever swam or winged across the stream, but which has always proved attractive to grayling.

On the evening of Bank Holiday I put on a Red Spinner—and thereby hangs a curious tale of a singular incident which befell "The A. A.," and but for which I should not have thought it worth my while to write anything about so insignificant an event as our summer visit to our pleasant river of unattractive name.

"Red Spinner" is the *nom de guerre* of a celebrated writer and angler, whose pseudonym I had once innocently maligned in a way which brought a mild remonstrance from him. Now, as the sequel will show, he hath his revenge. Red Spinner has justified the adjective I then applied to it, in a personal and very touching manner.

The little incident to which I have referred came about in this way—an incident which very narrowly escaped being a very serious, if not dangerous, accident : I had begun our evening fishing by catching a nice grayling in the pub. field, my spirits rising, as the grayling evidently were beginning to rise. I strode on up to the Leg of Mutton, and then I cast my Red Spinner over a big grayling that had just risen in mid-stream, but he declined the offer ; again he came up, and again I placed the Spinner on the point of his nose, so to speak, but he still declined. I was perhaps a little flustered at this contempt. I drew up hastily, and as I drew my foot slipped in a hole ; the consequence was that a gust of wind brought line and gut in a confused heap bang into my face ; there was no entanglement, for I threw it all out again straight over the still rising fish, but with the impression, delicately conveyed to my ears by the sound of the swish of my line, that the fly was off. I wound up accordingly, and I found that off it was, and I began making arrangements for putting on a fresh one. I called out to the Major—who was near by—and told him to have a go at my grayling while I replaced my lost fly.

"Lost your fly !" cried he, looking curiously into my face ; " why, it 's sticking in your nose !" And he burst into a roar of laughter.

Then I, wondering, put my finger to the tip of my nose ; not as the usual uncomplimentary mark of contempt, but really to find out whether or no his exclamation had any truth in it. And there, to my astonishment, my horror, and, I may add, my terror, I found the hook firmly embedded in the cartilage at the very point of my nose, with half an inch of gut attached to it. When I made the recast I must have driven the hook deeply into the nose, and far below the barb. The force of the throw is indicated by the fact that the gut had snapped. And yet, most marvellous thing of all, I never felt the slightest pang or twitch, and I was absolutely ignorant that the fly was where it was until my son exclaimed, " Why, it's in your nose ! "

I have on more than one occasion expressed some compunction on the score of giving pain to fish by hooking them by the lip or gill. I regard my own personal experience as a scientific solution of the problem—my doubts are now removed—if I, a full-blooded animal, can feel no pain when a hook is violently forced into the cartilage of my nose, how much less can a bloodless fish, with no sensorial nerve, be supposed to feel when gently drawn from his natural element and landed on the green sod ?

The Major, on examining the case more closely, took a more serious view of it than his first unseemly burst of hilarity indicated ; he saw that the hook was in deep below the barb, and that a surgical operation was necessary to get it out.

Of course we knocked off fishing at once,

much to our regret and disappointment, for it
was our last night, and the grayling were showing up.

Slowly and solemnly I marched home, cover-
ing up my face with my handkerchief whenever
I met anyone on the road. When I reached
the house I examined my nose in a looking-
glass, and I confess I felt woefully discouraged ;
the barbed-betrayer was there firmly fixed, and
I saw there was nothing for it but to send for
the doctor.

Our good friend M., the farmer, always ready
to help us in an emergency, at once drove off
three miles in search of one, and meanwhile I
managed to wash and brush up, and I sat down
to dinner with the hook in my nose, and with
the most gloomy forebodings as to what would
have to be done when the doctor arrived.

In about two hours he came, and found me
smoking a cigar, for, in spite of my misgivings,
I was determined to put a bold face on it. He
examined the position very carefully, shook his
head sadly, and said it was a very difficult, and
he feared painful, business. He thought at first
it would be possible to break off the eyed shank
of the hook, strip it of its feathers, and press the
whole hook through without the necessity of
cutting a hole in my nose ; but this was found
impracticable, he had no weapon strong enough
to cut the steel wire. A strong pair of scissors

was first tried, which made me feel, I fancy, something like what a bull may feel when they are putting a ring in his nose; but nothing came of it. The scissors were of no use. So said the doctor, "There is nothing for it but to use the lancet. It is but a small one, I shall not hurt you much. Bring me a basin of warm water and a sponge."

I pictured myself with my nose split open, and a gash that would be a mark for the remainder of my days, and my heart sank within me.

He seized my nose and the Red Spinner between the finger and thumb of his left hand, and with his right he began slashing away with his lovely little lancet. I bore it all manfully, although I thought surely he is cutting off the end of my nose! But really and truly, before I had time to cry "Jack Robinson" he had done the job, and gracefully handed me my Red Spinner, of which the Major took possession, and means to preserve it as a memento of what we all look upon as a singular and curious incident.

I cannot close this chapter without expressing my thanks to the young surgeon who so deftly performed this really delicate operation, for it will hardly be believed that he has scarcely left a mark behind him. A man who can perform so small an operation so perfectly may safely be intrusted with more serious work.

CHAPTER XIV.

ON THE EDGE OF EXMOOR.

EPTEMBER 8, 1897.—"The Flying Dutchman" flew with me from Paddington to Dulverton in four and a half hours, only stopping at Bath, Bristol, and Taunton—for a few minutes. It was a lovely morning, and so continued until we reached Taunton. Then it began and continued to rain for the remainder of the day and the following night; it ceased not until the next morning.

At Dulverton I was met by a good friend, my future host, with a dogcart; we started for a nine miles' drive in a torrent of rain. A little way out from Dulverton station, which is two miles from the town, we found the road blocked and impassable. There were probably sixty or seventy hunters—men, women, and boys—waiting at the foot of Allen's Wood for the stag to come down to the river; but it was getting late, and he came not, nor was the sound of horn or bark of

DULVERTON.

hound to be heard. They seemed confident, however, that down through the wood he would presently dash, and so in a downpour they waited, with more patience, perhaps, than politeness. We were blocked, and instead of moving they only gave us a grim stare. At last one of them, more considerate than the rest, shouted, "Make room there; surely these gentlemen have as much right to the public road as you." This remonstrance moved them, and they gradually formed a double row, leaving us room to pass between. They looked thoroughly soaked, and some of them woebegone; certainly it was a trying time for them—but so it was for us.

I came into this country to fish, not to hunt, and so I have not heard whether they killed on that occasion; but I was afterwards told by one of them, an enthusiastic hunter, that they made a record run four days later, on Saturday, the 11th. The stag led them right on to the rocks near Porlock, and got fixed on a ledge of rock, where the hounds could not reach him. Lord Ebrington tried to dislodge him. He climbed down to some point under the ledge where the deer was lodged, and had a very narrow escape indeed, for the deer, in his excitement, dislodged large blocks of rock, which came rolling down over his lordship's head. Fortunately, none of them touched him. He had, however, in his eagerness, reached a point from which he could not retreat, and they had to lower ropes for his rescue. I tell the tale as it was told to me, but as the "Field" correspondent was present, I have no doubt a more detailed and accurate account will be found in that paper. "Words," says the "West Somerset Free Press," "are inadequate to describe the entrancing beauty of the scene, as the stag, still panting, stood sharply defined against the clear blue sky, with liquid eye turned upon his clustering foes a hundred feet below, while three climbers slowly close on him with the dreaded rope—a real wild scene of a grandeur such as is rarely known in prosaic England, the whole lit up by the mellow rays of the September sun."

Two of the hounds lost their foothold on the yielding stone slides, and fell over the rocks. One of them was rescued, but "Old Cheshire Dreamer" will hunt no more.

To return to my own particular story. I may say that mine host, whom I had never met before, proved a very intelligent and interesting farmer. We drove through some very romantic scenery — all the time in a downpour. We travelled over Winsford Hill, where the Devil's Punch Bowl is—but as yet I have not seen it—and towards Exford, and finally he landed me at his home.

Here it was that I was met by the Professor, who had secured for me these pleasant

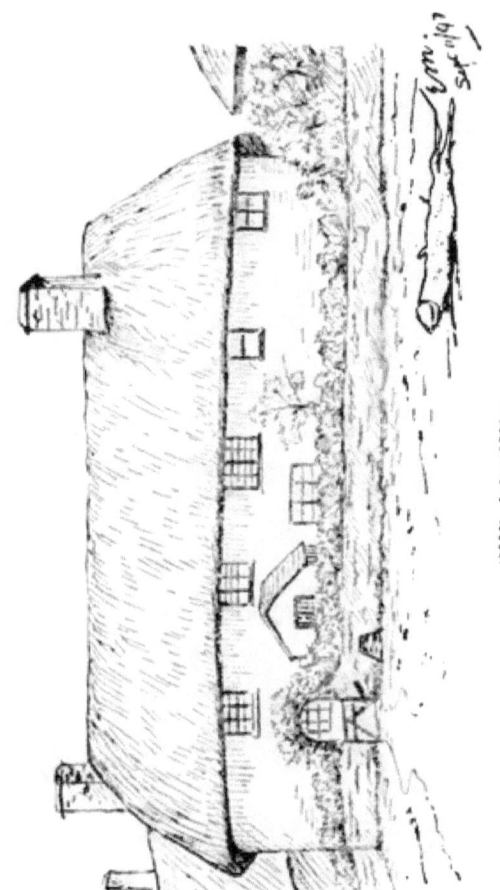

OUR DIGGINGS.

diggings, and who not only gave me the friend-
liest of greetings, but, as usual, had sacrificed
his own comfort by giving up his bedroom to
me, the best in the house. So here we are, nine
miles from the nearest station. The postman
climbs this hill (we are nine hundred feet above
the sea) only three days a week. The post-office
Jubilee regulations have not reached these parts
yet. If we want to communicate with the outside world oftener than this, we must trudge it
some three miles to the nearest post office.

Next morning, which was bright and splendid
after the previous month of rain, I was able to
take a general survey of my holiday quarters.

If all the world's a stage, and all the men and
women merely players, I have discovered in this
little corner of Somerset a special and peculiar
stage on which I can strut alone or in the Professor's company. My stage is of green grass,
my audience the green, beautiful, and silent
woods which surround my theatre ; my orchestra
the birds, and my music the running, roaring, or
bubbling river down yonder—three hundred
yards down a green precipitous slope, which
dips from the edge of my platform.

Yonder, far above the river and the woods,
but just on a level with my platform, floats
a great broad-winged buzzard ; still higher,
amongst the gods, as it were, up and beyond
the tops of the green woods, are cultivated fields

I

of corn and wheat not yet gathered. I assure
you it is the prettiest amphitheatre that ever was
seen.

This was my first acquaintance with the
buzzard, a bird well known here. He is to be
distinguished from the hawk by his size and
sedentary disposition. He is about twenty inches
in length, and four feet and a half in the spread
of his wings. His habit is to sit for many hours
perched on a tree or some eminence waiting for
bird, reptile, or quadruped which may come
within his reach.

My platform is backed up by a very picturesque old farmhouse—white walls, thatched
roof, with a low, long frontage, facing a very
pretty flower garden, daintily laid out with
dahlias, love-lies-bleeding, marigolds, and many
other autumn flowers and ferns. I have tried in
my clumsy way to give a sketch of the house.
It is rough and imperfect, and I suppose no one
would imagine that behind that hedge a pretty
garden lies. It is in this picture of a "fit
retreat of health and peace" that the good
farmer and his wife, son, and daughter have
been so obliging as to find me lodgings—for it *is*
a favour—and here the Professor and I are fixed
for a time, to enjoy the lovely scenery, and to
catch as many fish as we can in the Barle,
which meanders down yonder in and out amid
the green foliage.

THE BUZZARD.

(*Falco buteo.*)

A curious thing about this farm, so it seems to me, is that our old friend, the sparrow, is no-where to be seen. On the other hand, the place is alive with the songs of robins before sunrise, and on till long after sunset. Have the robins, which are quite numerous, driven the sparrows away?

The greater probability is that they had gone away to the stubbles, but as a matter of fact I was told that at no time are they numerous here. In the valley below an enthusiastic clergyman had estimated that at least a hundred different kinds of birds may be seen and heard in their seasons.

The first night of my abode in this solitary dwelling I was awoke in the small hours by a weird and unearthly shrieking at my window—the cry was something like *kirrwee, kirrwee!* It also disturbed the Professor on several occasions. I am familiar enough with the hooting of the common owl in the woods ; it was prob-ably a screech owl, or a moping owl that "does to the moon complain" ; at all events it was not comfortable to be aroused by such an ill-omened visitor.

So much for the surroundings. On the morn-ing of the 9th we took a genera. survey of the river in the immediate neighbourhood, and in the afternoon I cast my first fly over the river, and that was at once firmly fixed in an ash tree

across the stream, over a deep pool—there it
had to remain. That was my first lesson. The
fact is, however, the river just now is brimful,
and rushing along with rapid strength ; there is
no wading to be done, and to cast from the bank
between two alder or nut bushes that meet at
the top, with a shrubbery behind you, and bushes
or trees overhanging the water in front of you,
and a strongish wind blowing just the way it
ought not to blow, it is easily to be understood
how I got hung up before I became acquainted
with the habits and customs of this sprightly
river. I caught one trout, and the Professor
caught none, for it is not always given to the
wise and prudent to catch fish here—babes and
sucklings in the art sometimes beat them.

On Friday, the 10th, a lovely bright day, I
toiled all day in the hot sun and caught nothing.
The Professor caught two brace. There was no
rise ; wind north-easterly. We fished from the
bottom of Bradley Ham to Withypool. River
still too strong to wade. The Professor is good
at climbing alders and dislodging flies from the
topmost branches with a hook and spike fixed at
the end of his net handle, an ingenious arrange-
ment of his own contrivance, and I kept him
pretty well employed in this exercise. On one
occasion I sent him, or I had better say his un-
bounded enthusiasm sent him, to climb an un-
usually tall and bushy alder, and my fly was in

the topmost branch. It is not easy to climb far up an alder, for the branches are slender and snappish. He had got up almost near enough to reach my fly with his hook, when the brittle branch on which he was resting for support gave way, and down he came, but caught by the branches under both arms, and so he hung suspended over the water for some time. He soon struggled out of his troubles and landed on the firm earth, but not until he had rescued my " Coachman." The adventure shook him a good deal. It was a glorious day—the scenery in its infinite variety of hills and woods and shades and colours quite enough to satisfy me without the mere secondary consideration of catching a few trout. I suppose that is why I was not eminently successful.

The next day, Sept. 11, we started early. We had a long day before us. Our host very kindly devoted his valuable time to our service by driving us in the morning to some distance above Withypool, and leaving us there to fish up the river, Landacre Bridge way.

Here was another delightful day. We fished upstream with more success, for the river is more open and accessible, and had lowered now sufficiently to enable us to wade here and there, and so to reach spots where the trout lay. Consequently, when lunch time came, which we partook of under the wide-spreading branches of a lovely beech, we had each a fair show of pretty trout—small, of course, for there are no large ones. This, I may remark, is the country of beech trees. The hedgerows are all beech, and capital, impenetrable hedges they make, as we occasionally found. We came upon one which ran from the top of a hill sheer down to the very edge of the water—we must either climb that hill to reach an opening or get round the water end of it. Now, this lower corner of the field was a bog, and through the bog we had to struggle to get to the end of the hedge.

The Professor is generally the first to tackle any difficulty, but he did not like this job, so I led the way, and a nasty job it was. I squeezed through thick bushes to the water's edge, and then found myself suspended by a few roots and brittle branches over an abrupt precipice of six feet above the water, which happened to be one of the deepest holes in the river. I held on, rod and net in one hand, sometimes grasping green ferns, which snapped easily, then by seizing young ash or beech branches, I clambered through. The Professor was not quite so lucky. Just when he had reached the most dangerous part his right foot slipped, and he found himself hanging over the gulf below with only one foot resting on a rotten root and his hands grasping whatever they could seize ; but he got through all right after an anxious struggle.

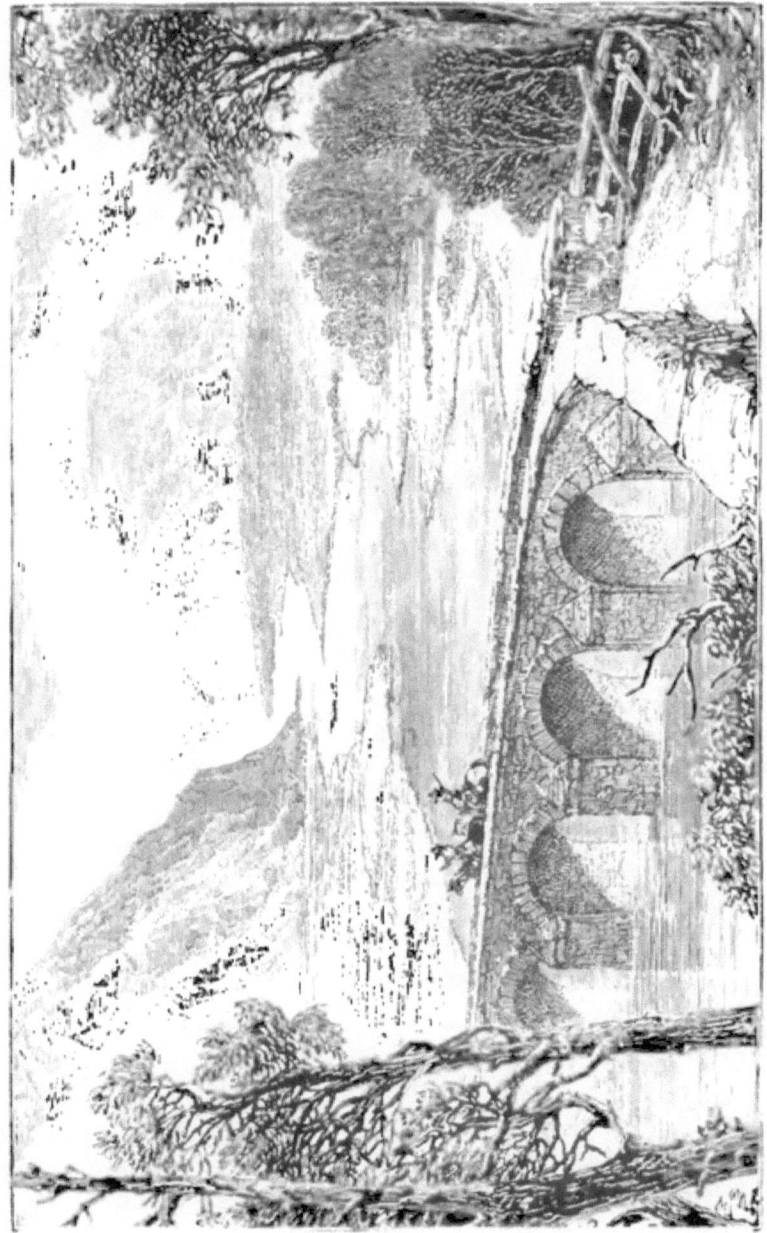

Then we fished on up Landacre way till we came to the bridge—a very picturesque bridge of six arches, of which I am enabled to give an admirable picture from the illustrated edition of " Lorna Doone." Here it was that Jeremy Stickles had a fight for life—first with the great floods that came down over the bridge, and then with the three Doones. This illustration is from a drawing by a local celebrity (Mr. F. Armstrong). It realizes the scene perfectly.

Here it is an understood thing that, although the fishing ticket issued by the Exe Conservancy Board embraces the waters of the Exe and its tributaries in the counties of Devon and Somerset, a certain formality has to be gone through at this bridge in order to appease the owner of this particular property. This formality consists in walking up a steep hill on the South Molton turnpike road, to Landacre House, where you have to sign your name in a book kept there for that purpose. Under ordinary circumstances this would not be a very pleasant performance, for it is no joke to climb such a hill as this in heavy wading boots, after having walked for many miles up the river. But to us, notwithstanding these troubles (and we were almost exhausted when we reached the house), it was a peculiar pleasure, because the farmer and his wife, Mr. and Mrs. Hill, and Miss Milton are all old friends of the Professor. Consequently, we were well entertained with most acceptable refreshments. Miss Milton told me that she was born in that house, and her father lived there for ninety years.

In turning over the leaves of the old book in which we recorded our names, it was with a peculiar sensation that I came across two names not unknown, and, I may say, very dear to me. The date was September, 1873—just twenty-four years ago ; the names were R. B. Marston (the "Major" of my booklets) and his brother, E. P. Marston. This Landacre House is a very interesting old farmhouse, and is situated on the side of a hill, which commands grand views over Withypool Common and Exmoor, the sides of which, here and there, show signs of having been cultivated in times gone by, when wheat and oats were worth growing. The river here runs broad and rapid, and free from encumbrance of trees and bushes—quite open, but by no means free from a greater nuisance in the way of bogs and swamps, which make the approaches to the water sometimes inconvenient. We returned to our pleasant residence, which is not to be reached from any point without considerable exertion.

In the evening, sitting round a cheerful fire, we consulted our hosts as to the best way to get across country to view the Doone Valley—which is supposed to be some fourteen or fifteen miles away—and it was finally agreed that he should drive us over on the Monday or Tuesday following. Our host told us, with a merry twinkle, that he had not read " Lorna Doone," and so was not acquainted with John Ridd ; " but," said he, " I have often heard tell of one Ambrose Ridd, who was a giant in his day. He may have been the father or the uncle or the cousin of John. In those days, and, indeed, in my own time, I remember well when there were no wheels to be seen in this country. My father was the first to introduce them. Everything was carried on the backs of horses in great sacks—lime, corn, wool, etc. On yonder hill are still to be seen the old packhorse roads. Well, this Ambrose Ridd had a load of wool 240 lb. for South Molton Fair. He scorned the use of horseflesh, and so took the sack on his back and trudged over hill and dale to South Molton. In passing through a gate on a common the tail end of his sack was hooked to the gate, probably by his Satanic Majesty,[1] but, quite unaware of this, Ambrose still trudged on, and when he reached his destination the people were astonished to see the gate still hanging on behind, and Ambrose was as much surprised as they were."

Sunday, Sept. 12.—My good friend the Pro-

[1] Bewick has a tailpiece representing his majesty engaged in a similar performance.

fessor, being a staunch churchman, took me away on foot to Withypool Church, in which church he has a special and peculiar interest. Some eighteen years ago the tower of the old church showed signs of danger, and it was decided to pull it down, and down they pulled two-thirds of it, when they found the stonework so solid and so hard that nothing less than dynamite could move it, and so there it remains in this tumble-down state to this day. The church itself was also in a sad ruinous state, and so ten years ago my active friend, the Professor, set about and organized subscriptions for the restoration. He constituted himself architect, surveyor, and clerk of the works. He devoted himself heart and soul to the work, besides contributing largely towards the cost, and so, with the active assistance of the farmers in the neighbourhood, he completed the renovation of the interior in a very elegant and tasteful manner. But as regards the tower, there it remains as it was when pulled down years ago, the stones piled up along the sides of the churchyard, whilst the part still standing has been roughly covered in. Pitiful it is to see, for the old church is splendidly situated, and forms, or rather will form when its new tower is built, a most picturesque object in the landscape. Why does not some millionaire in the county take it in hand and find the money, it requires only a few hundreds, and it would be a good deed to perform?

One of the Professor's friends whom we met at church, learning that we were bent on an expedition in search of the Doone Valley, very kindly offered to drive us there; and as he had been stag-hunting over there the day before, and knew the best road, we accepted his kind offer. And so our friend and host was, I think, a little disappointed that he was superseded.

On Monday, the 13th, nothing occurred of consequence, except that, fishing up Bradley Ham way I broke the top joint. I had hold of a good trout ($\frac{1}{2}$ lb.), which is as big as they are made in these rivers. This trout gave me no end of trouble, scuttling about from one boulder to another; and it was in pulling him out from under a rock that my rod snapped, but I managed to bag my trout. I was helpless, for I had no string, or wax, or anything to make a splice with, and so I had to whistle for the Professor. He soon turned up—sliced a piece of tough young ash, drew forth from his capacious pockets just the string that was wanted, and also the necessary wax, and in a jiffy my rod was restored to working order. We fished on up the Ham till the appointed time for return had arrived. Then, punctual to the minute, our host came down the hillside with a couple of ponies to carry the fatigued and weary and hungry anglers back home. We rode the ponies, and our host trudged all the way back. He is a much older man than I, and I felt considerable compunction in allowing him to walk whilst I was riding his beautiful four-year-old cob "Progress"; but, in truth, I was so exhausted and footsore, that a three miles' walk over those hills after fishing and wading all day in heavy indiarubber soled boots would have been pain and grief to me. I cannot recommend such soles for such a rocky stream, for they are as slippery as eels. The Professor wore leather waders, with rough nailed leather soles. With these he could safely grip stones over which I was constantly stumbling.

CHAPTER XV.

THE DOONE VALLEY.

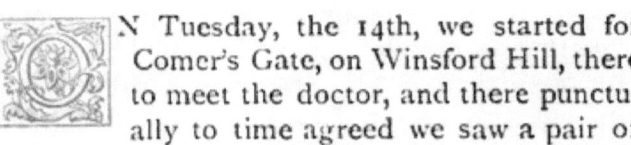N Tuesday, the 14th, we started for
Comer's Gate, on Winsford Hill, there
to meet the doctor, and there punctu-
ally to time agreed we saw a pair of
splendid grays come prancing over the hill.
The doctor drove his own horses, but had hired
a commodious wagonette, and in this carriage
was an enormous basket, occupying a fourth of
its whole length, and in this basket was contained—but I am not going to tell what it contained—and sitting next to this restaurant on
wheels, on each side, were two charming young
ladies—Mrs. E. and her niece—and next them
sat a fine cockaded and liveried groom, and still
there was room for us—pilgrims of the moor—
the Professor occupying the box seat.

I might also have said that the carriage was
freighted with a still more important personage
than any I have yet mentioned—the pet darling

of the ladies and the idol of the doctor. He was
a little black thing, with prominent eyes, an
abnormally big forehead, betraying wonderful
intelligence, if not water on the brain. He had
four little spindles for legs, and he weighed just
3 lb. He was not quite the sort of being for ex-
ploring the wildest part of Exmoor ; but it was
considered impossible to leave him behind on
account of his extraordinary ability for getting
into trouble. Sometimes he would get faceache
or toothache, or lumbago, or half choke himself
with a chicken bone. He wore a white coat,
trimmed with scarlet (if I remember rightly), and
he reposed and dozed quietly on the lap of his
mistress the whole journey. In fact, he behaved
in a quite gentlemanly way all the time. He
was all smiles and caresses, and knew nothing
of snapping or snarling, or barking and biting ;
and so we travelled, up hill and down dale, till we
came to Larksborough, a lone old farmhouse
and stabling, all in a state of dilapidation and
ruin, the house being now occupied by a Scotch
shepherd. Our splendid team had done this
rough work as if they had been used to it all
their lives, whereas, in fact, they had been more
used to the King's Road, Brighton. The groom
found stabling for them of some sort, and as
they carried their own provisions they were soon
made happy.

Now, here we are landed in the very centre of

Exmoor—as wild and dreary a country as could
be seen, and we had to trudge the remainder of
the way. Just down below us is a small gutter,
through which some water trickles; it is the
head water of Badgworthy River. We had now
to follow this stream, which gradually grew into
a respectable brook, for three or four, or perhaps
five, miles, before it reaches that renowned fall
up which John Ridd climbed and found Lorna
on the top of it. We kept the brook in view,
though sometimes climbing over hilltops and
crossing goyals. We had travelled in this way
about three miles, when Mrs. E. began to think
that it was too fatiguing for her little darling,
and so she sat down on the hillside waiting our
return. She was, I am sure, in mortal fear all
the time lest a rabbit should cross her path. In
that case the spirit of her darling would be irre-
pressible. He would burst his bonds and be
after that rabbit, and then if he caught him there
was the terrible possibility that the rabbit might
eat him! The consequence of all this was that
the little tyrant had to be wrapped up and coddled
all the time we were away.

We pushed along our course over hill and dale
for about a mile further, the young lady tripping
it over the rocks and swamps just as Lorna herself might have done, and never owning to be
the least bit tired. We crossed the foot of
Thomshill, a place which, according to " Lorna

Doone," "folk were loth to speak of even on a summer morning ; that Squire Thom, who had been murdered there a century ago or more, had been seen by several shepherds, even in the middle of the day, walking with his severed head carried in his left hand, and his right arm lifted towards the sun."

We reached a point called the Hut Circles, three hillocks, very picturesquely situated, and each of them covered with heaps of stone, which had once doubtless formed huts. But it seemed clear that as yet we had only reached the head of the Doone Valley, which extends for three or four miles down. Perhaps we had reached the spot where it was easy to imagine the young Lord Alan Brandir met his tragic fate at the hands of Carver Doone. In order to get further down it was necessary to cross the stream, which now ran strong and full, and there is no bridge. We were obliged to give it up for the present, fully intending to return another day and attack the valley from another point.

We have not seen all we wanted to see, for it is hard and toilsome work on a very hot day to climb up and down these rocky hills ; and it became evident that we must pursue " The Badgery " two or three miles further before we can get into our minds a realistic picture of the Doone Valley.

The great " Wizard of the West " has cast

such a glamour of romance and unreality over the glen of the Doones, that one's discovery of the real valley may turn out to be somewhat disappointing. My next expedition, if I am ever permitted to make another, will be first to discover Plover's Barrows, and so follow John Ridd over the track of that singular loach fishing expedition, which had such astounding consequences. I have much pleasure in being able to give an excellent picture of Plover's Barrows, by Mr. F. G. Armstrong, from the illustrated edition of "Lorna Doone." Therein will be seen the River Lynn winding through the hills, down which John Ridd (when he was turned fourteen, and put into small clothes, buckled at the knee) went a-loaching with a three-pronged fork fastened to a stout rod. Two miles down it is joined by the Badgworthy, up which John went, and "had very comely sport," till he came to the water slide, which landed him in the Doone Valley. Useless now for any bold young angler to expect to find loach in either of these streams—John Ridd exterminated them.

During our drive back the admired and beloved miniature Jumbo behaved in most becoming manner, and was the centre of admiration of all on board. We had a most delightful day, and felt very grateful to our friends for giving us the pleasure of their pleasant company, and for our share in their carriage.

K

The next day, the 15th, we began our fishing at Withypool, where on our return we should find a brace of nags to convey our weary bones back home. The most that can be said of it is that it was, as usual, a pleasant day. I shot ahead of the Professor ; and, as I was approaching the part of the river on which Landacre House looks down from a considerable distance, I heard the furious barking of dogs, and three big sheep-dogs came tearing down the meadows. I was puzzled to know what they were after, but on rounding a corner of the hill I descried away off in the distance to my left, that is, on the crest of Withypool Common, a solitary horseman, making his way slantingly towards the South Moulton Road, which stretches away up over Exmoor from Landacre Bridge. This horseman was immediately followed by many more. They came over the crest by the dozen, and galloped off in the same direction. Others came up from the other side down by Landacre House, and galloped over the bridge and up the road, making for the top, and there on the crest of the distant hill scores of them stood, seemingly not knowing which way to go, but gradually they vanished from my sight and I saw no more of them. I suppose the stag and hounds had gone over before I heard the farm dogs bark, and so I missed what must have been a very picturesque sight.

My business is to fish, not to hunt, but really I should have been delighted with "Progress" under me to have followed those gallant hunters. I toiled back till I found the Professor, who had given me up for lost. We caught a good many trout that day. A worthy dweller in Withypool, always alert for odd jobs so long as they don't mean real work, who answers to the name of Luke, brought our walking boots up to meet us, and gladly we exchanged our heavy waders and walked back to the Royal Oak. Here we found the place crowded with hunters whose horses had become blown and had given up the chase. They were all crying out for gruel or bran mash for their horses, and we had a difficulty in getting our steeds ready. At last we mounted, fishing rods in hand. Don Quixote-like we charged the hill in front of us. Heavily laden we were, and not quite in hunting trim. But away up yonder gallops a redcoat, said by the knowing ones to be Mr. Anthony, the popular huntsman, followed by a few other riders. This gallant stag—a galloper they call him—must have led them a pretty chase, for it was several hours since I had seen the hunters disappear over the Western Hill, and now here they are still pursuing over yonder Eastern Hill towards Winsford.

He was started in the morning in Hawkridge Covert, off by South Hill Cottages to Withypool,

and away then west by Knighton Combe and
Brightworthy Barrows to Delacombe and Kings-
land Pitts, West Molland Coverts, and at last
back up by Bradley and Comer's Gate. Our
route took us up to Comer's Gate and across
Winsford Hill, and when we got up there the
shades of evening were closing around us. But
my plucky " Progress " stood still, lifted his head
—ears forward—and neighed. Then he wanted
to be off. He had heard at a great distance the
sound of horses galloping over the heath, and he
longed to follow. I only caught sight of one
hunter, who soon disappeared towards the
Devil's Punch Bowl, and I managed to keep
" Progress " in the way he should go, for it
would not be a pretty picture to see me, fishing
rod and net in hand, two big baskets on my
back, galloping after the hounds. I am sure
" Progress " would have been off had the hounds
come in view. They had a most exciting run
of over thirty miles, but the stag did them at
last— he was driven to soil in King's Weir,
where he was lost in the dark.

I do not feel it to be incumbent on me to
describe the flies mostly successful on this water.
We tried a variety, some good, some not ; but
the fly for this river, I was confidently told by
an old hand, is one which neither I nor my experienced friend, the Professor, have yet seen.
He called it the Devon Green. Will some good

reader, who knows it, be good enough to state what are its constituent parts? It is, I believe, specially intended for greenhorns or green hands.

From what I hear, I fancy the trees and bushes which encompass the Barle in the wooded valleys are hung with as many "imitations" as there are real flies on the water. I am not the only one who got "hung up."

Thursday, 16th, was a dull, cold day. The Professor laboured hard at the stream, and brought home a good dish of trout. I fished only for an hour, and, not feeling well, I gave it up. Next day, 17th, heavy rain all day. I rested at home to recruit.

On Saturday, 18th, we fished in the afternoon up Withypool way, and caught a few nice trout under difficulties, for we had a storm of thunder and lightning and heavy rain, followed by a hailstorm, and afterwards a strong wind.

On Sunday, 19th, we walked across country to see the wonderful Torr Steps (formerly called Tarr Steps), built over the Barle, not far from Hawkridge, by his Satanic Majesty, according to "Lorna Doone"; but another tradition is that it was built by a man of the name of Tarr centuries ago. The enormous blocks of stone are supposed to have been dug out of the rocky bed of the river a few yards above ; at all events, there is a great pool there where the salmon lie.

Many years ago, one dark night, the Professor, accompanied by our "Major," met with a singular adventure here. They had been spending the evening with the late rector close by, and were crossing this river, homeward bound, on a very dark night by this bridge of steps, when the Professor slipped and fell plump on his back into a deepish hole in the river. The Major went into the stream and got him out. The Professor had a quantity of loose silver and a half-sovereign in his pocket, and these coins all fell into the water. Next morning they went down to the place, and by much groping in the bright water recovered the treasure; the half-sovereign hangs on the Major's watch-chain as a memento to this day. The Professor showed me the exact spot where the accident happened; lucky for him that the back of his head just escaped a big rock that stands up there above the water.

The Rectory of Hawkridge and Withypool combined stands in a romantic spot a few hundred yards above the river—five miles away from one parish and two from the other. We spent a pleasant hour there.

On Monday, the 20th, the morning was fine, but windy. We ought to have gone on another expedition in search of the Doone Valley, but our steeds were not available. On our route we should have passed Larksborough, on Exmoor, and there we should have witnessed a lively scene, for there was an assemblage of two or three thousand people to witness what they call Point-to-Point races—a five miles' run across the moor from Larksborough to Simonsbath. I did not hear what the result was ; but two of the consequences were that a rider fell and broke his collar-bone, and a horse had his leg broken, and was promptly shot. It must have been a lively scene on that wild spot, in the wildest part of Exmoor.

Tuesday and Wednesday were devoted to the quiet and peaceful recreation of angling, with fair results, and on Thursday I am homeward bound. This little spell of outdoor life was very pleasant for me and very healthful, but all too short, for I enjoyed everything with the exuberant feelings of a boy, though an old one —my pleasant residence, my pleasant, humorous, and delightful companion, the delicious Devonshire cream and whortleberries, and, above all, Devonshire junket, otherwise named by the Professor " Patent slip down " ! all of which were prepared for us by our venerable hostess and her charming, sprightly, bright-eyed daughter.

On my return homewards over Winsford Hill, we made a short detour to get a glimpse of the far-famed Devil's Punch Bowl, which is quite worth going a long way to see. It looks like an enormous scallop taken bodily out of the side of

the mountain. I had only time to get a peep
over the rim. It is more in the shape of a horse-
shoe than a bowl, three parts of it being quite
circular, and the fourth opening out to the valley
below, looking northward. I will not hazard a
guess as to the number of hundreds of feet of its
depth, or as to its circumference. Its sides are
of grass and fern, but I should think it would be
perilous to attempt its descent.

Our sanguine expectations of October grayling
fishing on the Itchen have, alas! come to
nought. The Major had serious illness in his
family, and I was otherwise prevented. That
big trout which our Major hooked and lost in
May, with a hook and two yards of gut attached
to him, still remains in his lair; let us hope that
we shall find him in the full enjoyment of health
and freedom, with a pound added to his weight,
when the spring-time comes.

THE KESTREL.

(Falco tinnunculus.)

CHAPTER XVI.

" FAMILIAR WILD BIRDS." [1]

THESE handy little volumes are most charming. In the first place they contain about one hundred and fifty exquisitely printed coloured plates of as many "Familiar Wild Birds," and innumerable little woodcuts such as the specimens I am enabled to give by the kindness of the publishers. As to the coloured plates a practical angler might be tempted to put each of these lovely birds—dressed as they are in their natural plumage—under a microscope, in order to see what feathers from breast, wing, or throat would make the most killing imitations of winged insects wherewith to deceive the lordly trout or thymy grayling. But this was not the object which Mr. Swaysland had in view when he got Mr. Thorburn to make these exquisite pictures.

[1] "Familiar Wild Birds." By W. Swaysland. In four crown 8vo volumes.

They are intended to enable us who are not ornithologists, but who love all the birds we meet with in our wanderings, to distinguish them by their familiar names. For myself, I may say that my early boyhood was spent "by meadow and stream." In lovely woods and by pleasant rivers I made acquaintance with very many of the Familiar Birds here so accurately depicted, and I knew them by their local names, sometimes differing from those given here, *e.g.*, for the Redstart our name was Brantail, etc. An interval of sixty years is "the difference 'twixt *now* and then," and in that interval my woodland wanderings have been of rare occurrence. I have forgotten the names of many birds, and these pretty volumes bring back to me not only forgotten names but pleasant memories of days gone by. These coloured plates are wonderfully accurate, not only in the colours of the plumage, but in delineament of shape and attitude of each bird, and there is at foot of each a note showing the proportion of size which the picture bears to the original bird.

Mr. Swaysland's text is as useful and as interesting as are his pictures. In addition to the coloured plates, the text is liberally interspersed with pretty woodcuts, which add much to the attraction of the volumes.

In the text the most persistent, prosy, practical angler might learn to distinguish a black-

THE CREEPER.

(*Certhia familiaris.*)

bird from a starling, a swallow from a sand martin, or a swift from a leather-bat, and would come to know in time that birds are far more interesting beings than fishes. Mr. Swaysland tells you all you want to know about them, their habits, their migration, how and where they build their nests, and the colour, markings, and size of their eggs, with much more useful information.

If I could find it in my heart to blame these volumes for anything, it would be because the birds are not assorted—they are thrown together anyhow—thus the shorelark is found in one place, the skylark in another, and the woodlark in another, and so with the buntings, and many others. I am at a loss to know why birds of a feather were not brought together.

It is true that when I come to the end of vol. 4 I find an excellent classified index, in which the birds are all brought together according to their scientific affinities. There is also what I must venture to call a very bad general index, under which I can find neither bunting, nor sandpiper, nor snipe, nor wren, nor wagtail, nor probably a score of other familiar names. If I want bunting, I must look to *black-headed* or *common*, and I must search all through the index before I can find anything about a snipe or a wren.

I strongly advise Mr. Swaysland to cancel this index and substitute a decent one for it.

This small defect being remedied, I have nothing but praise for these volumes, and can very sincerely commend them to the attention of all who are not, but who wish to become, familiar with the names as well as the bodily presentment of all the birds that haunt our woods and streams.

CHISWICK PRESS:—CHARLES WHITTINGHAM AND CO.
TOOKS COURT, CHANCERY LANE, LONDON.

EDITION DE LUXE, *in 2 Vols. Royal 4to, each copy numbered and signed, to Subscribers, Ten Guineas net (nearly all sold).*

The DEMY QUARTO EDITION, *bound in half-morocco, gilt top, Five Guineas net.*

WALTON AND COTTON'S
THE COMPLEAT ANGLER.

THE LEA AND DOVE ILLUSTRATED EDITION.

(THE 100TH EDITION.)

EDITED BY R. B. MARSTON.

The principal feature of this Edition is a Set of 54 Full-page Photogravures, printed from Copper Plates, on fine Plate Paper, of Views on the Lea, Dove, &c., and about 100 other Illustrations.

"The edition which celebrates the centenary of 'The Compleat Angler' is altogether worthy of the immortal work. Mr. Marston, the Editor of the 'Fishing Gazette,' who is known as a 'deacon of the craft,' has grudged neither time, nor money, nor labour in perfecting these two magnificent volumes. The wide and practical knowledge of the publisher has gratified and satisfied the sympathies of the editor. The type and paper make a masterpiece of mechanical work, and the exquisite photogravures with which the volumes are embellished leave little or nothing to be desired."—*The Times.*

"The noblest gift-book that has been issued for many years."—*St. James's Gazette.*

Some Important Angling Works.

[New Volume of "The Book Lover's Library."] £.]

WALTON AND SOME EARLIER WRITERS ON FISH AND FISHING. By R. B. MARSTON, Editor of "The Fishing Gazette." Printed on antique paper, in cloth bevelled, with rough edges, price 4s. 6d. Printed on handmade paper, in Roxburghe, half-morocco, with gilt top; 250 only are printed, for sale in England, price 7s. 6d. Large Paper edition, on handmade paper. (All sold.)

A HISTORY OF SCANDINAVIAN FISHES. Described by B. FRIES, C. Y. EKSTRÖM, and C. SUNDEVALL. With Coloured Plates painted from Living Specimens, and Engraved on Stone by WILHELM VON WRIGHT, besides numerous Text Illustrations. Second Edition. Thoroughly Revised and Completed by Professor F. A. SMITT, Member of the Royal Swedish Academy of Science. In Two Parts, price £12 12s. net.

FAVOURITE FLIES AND THEIR HISTORIES. By MARY ORVIS MARBURY. With many Replies from Practical Anglers to Inquiries concerning How, When, and Where to use them. Illustrated by Thirty-two Coloured Plates of Flies, Six Engravings of Natural Insects, and Eight Reproductions of Photographs. Fully Illustrated. 8vo, cloth extra, 24s.

HOW TO TIE SALMON FLIES. A Treatise on the Methods of Tying the various kinds of Salmon Flies. With about Seventy entirely new Wood Engravings, and containing the Dressing of Forty Flies. By CAPTAIN HALE, East Lancashire Regiment. Demy 8vo, cloth extra, 12s. 6d.

"Will be prized by everyone who uses it."—*Scotsman*.

Some Important Angling Works—*cont.*

THE RIVERSIDE NATURALIST. Notes on the Various Forms of Life met with either in, on, or by the Water, or in its immediate vicinity. By EDWARD HAMILTON, M.D., F.L.S., &c., Author of "Recollections of Fly-fishing for Salmon, Trout, and Grayling," &c. With numerous Illustrations. Demy 8vo, cloth, 14s.

> "The volume should occupy a handy place on the shelves of every angling club in the kingdom."—*The Field.*

THAMES AND TWEED. By GEORGE ROOPER. Crown 8vo, cloth, 2s. 6d.

THE FLY-FISHER'S REGISTER. By W. H. POPE. Half bound, size 13 in. by 8 in., 4s.

FLY TYING. By JAMES OGDEN. Illustrated. 2s. 6d.

THE BRITISH ANGLER'S LEXICON. By RICHARD NEVIN. Illustrated. Crown 8vo, cloth extra, 5s.

NEAR AND FAR: AN ANGLER'S SKETCHES OF HOME SPORT AND COLONIAL LIFE. By WM. SENIOR ("Red Spinner"), Angling Editor of the *Field*, Author of "Waterside Sketches," &c. New and Cheaper Edition. Crown 8vo, boards, 2s.

WATERSIDE SKETCHES. By "Red Spinner" (WM. SENIOR). Imp. 32mo, boards, 1s.

THE SPORTING FISH OF GREAT BRITAIN. By H. CHOLMONDELEY-PENNELL. Illustrated by Sixteen Lithographs of Fish in Gold, Silver, and Colours. Demy 8vo, 15s.

MODERN IMPROVEMENTS IN FISHING TACKLE AND FISH HOOKS. By H. CHOLMONDELEY-PENNELL. With Two Hundred Illustrations. Crown 8vo, cloth, 2s.

Some Important Angling Works—*cont.*

NORTH COUNTRY TROUT FLIES. By T. E. PRITT. With Coloured Plates of all the best Flies. Second Edition. Demy 8vo, cloth, 10s. 6d.

A HANDY GUIDE TO DRY-FLY FISHING. By COTSWOLD ISYS, M.A. Illustrated. Third and Revised Edition. Crown 8vo, boards, 1s.

"A pretty discourse on various forms of dry-fly fishing . . . a series of clearly defined exercises."—*The Field.*

THE AMERICAN SALMON FISHERMAN. By HENRY P. WELLS. Illustrated. 116 pages. Small post 8vo, cloth, 6s.

FLY RODS AND FLY TACKLE. Suggestions for Amateurs as to their Manufacture and Use. By HENRY P. WELLS. Illustrated. Small 4to, 364 pages, cloth extra, 10s. 6d.

RECOLLECTIONS OF FLY-FISHING FOR SALMON, TROUT, AND GRAYLING. By EDWARD HAMILTON, M.D., F.L.S., &c. Illustrated. New Edition. Small post 8vo, cloth extra, 6s.

SALMON PROBLEMS. By J. W. WILLIS BUND. Boards, 2s. 6d.; cloth, 3s. 6d.

DOMESTICATED TROUT: HOW TO BREED AND GROW THEM. By LIVINGSTON STONE, United States Deputy Fish Commissioner. Price 5s.

AN ANGLER'S STRANGE EXPERIENCES. By COTSWOLD ISYS, M.A. Profusely Illustrated. Small 4to, cloth extra. Second and Cheaper Edition, 3s. 6d.

HOW AND WHERE TO FISH IN IRELAND. By HI REGAN. With Map and numerous Text Illustrations. Fifth Edition. Crown 8vo, 3s. 6d.

NOTES ON FISH AND FISHING. By J. J. MANLEY, M.A. With Illustrations. Crown 8vo, cloth extra, 363 pages, leatherette binding, 6s.

Some Important Angling Works—*cont.*

FLOAT FISHING AND SPINNING IN THE NOTTINGHAM STYLE. By J. W. MARTIN, the "Trent Otter." Coloured boards, Illustrated. Crown 8vo, 2s. 6d. New, Revised, and Enlarged Edition.

BRITISH ANGLING FLIES. By MICHAEL THEAKSTON. Revised and Annotated by FRANCIS M. WALBRAN. With Woodcut Illustrations, and Plates of Natural Flies drawn from Life. Crown 8vo, cloth, 5s.

THE LOWER AND MID THAMES : HOW AND WHERE TO FISH IT. By F. H. AMPHLETT. Crown 8vo, boards, 1s.

FISHING WITH THE FLY. Sketches by Lovers of the Art. With Coloured Illustrations of Standard Flies, collected by C. F. ORVIS and A. NELSON CHENEY. Square 8vo, cloth extra, 12s. 6d.

TALES FROM THE TELLING HOUSE.

By R. D. BLACKMORE, Author of "Lorna Doone," &c. Crown 8vo, with decorated Title-page, tastefully bound, cloth, gilt top, 5s.

*** The Stories are respectively entitled "SLAIN BY THE DOONES"; "FRIDA; or, the Lover's Leap"; "GEORGE BOWRING"; and "CROCKER'S HOLE."

The World says :—" Very good stories are these, especially "Slain by the Doones," in which John Ridd figures anew ; and a Legend of the West Country, "Frida, or the Lover's Leap," with beautiful passages of prose poetry in one of the saddest tales of woman's love and man's leaving that has ever been written."

www.ingramcontent.com/pod-product-compliance
Lightning Source LLC
Chambersburg PA
CBHW030601040726
47497CB00008B/2814